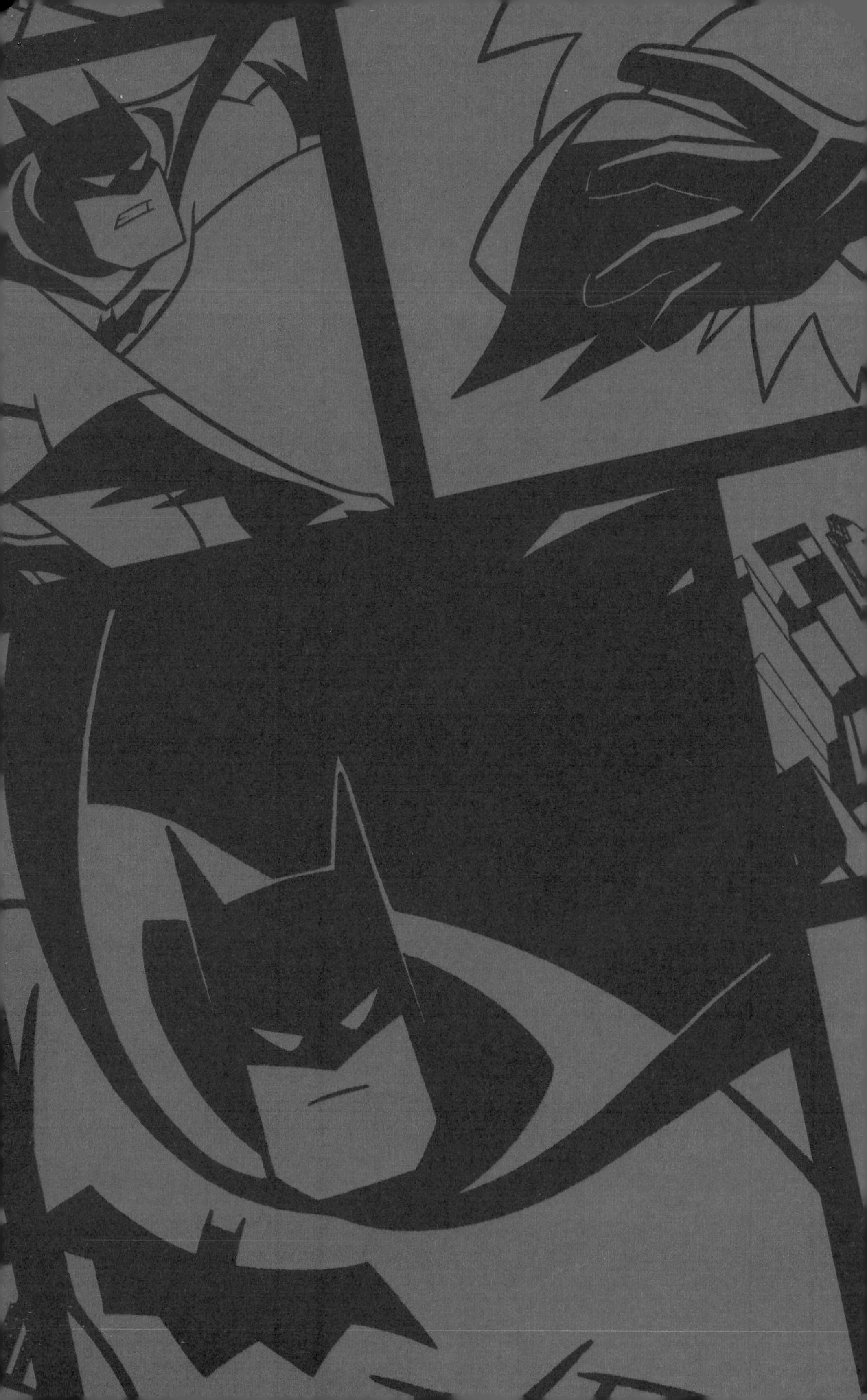

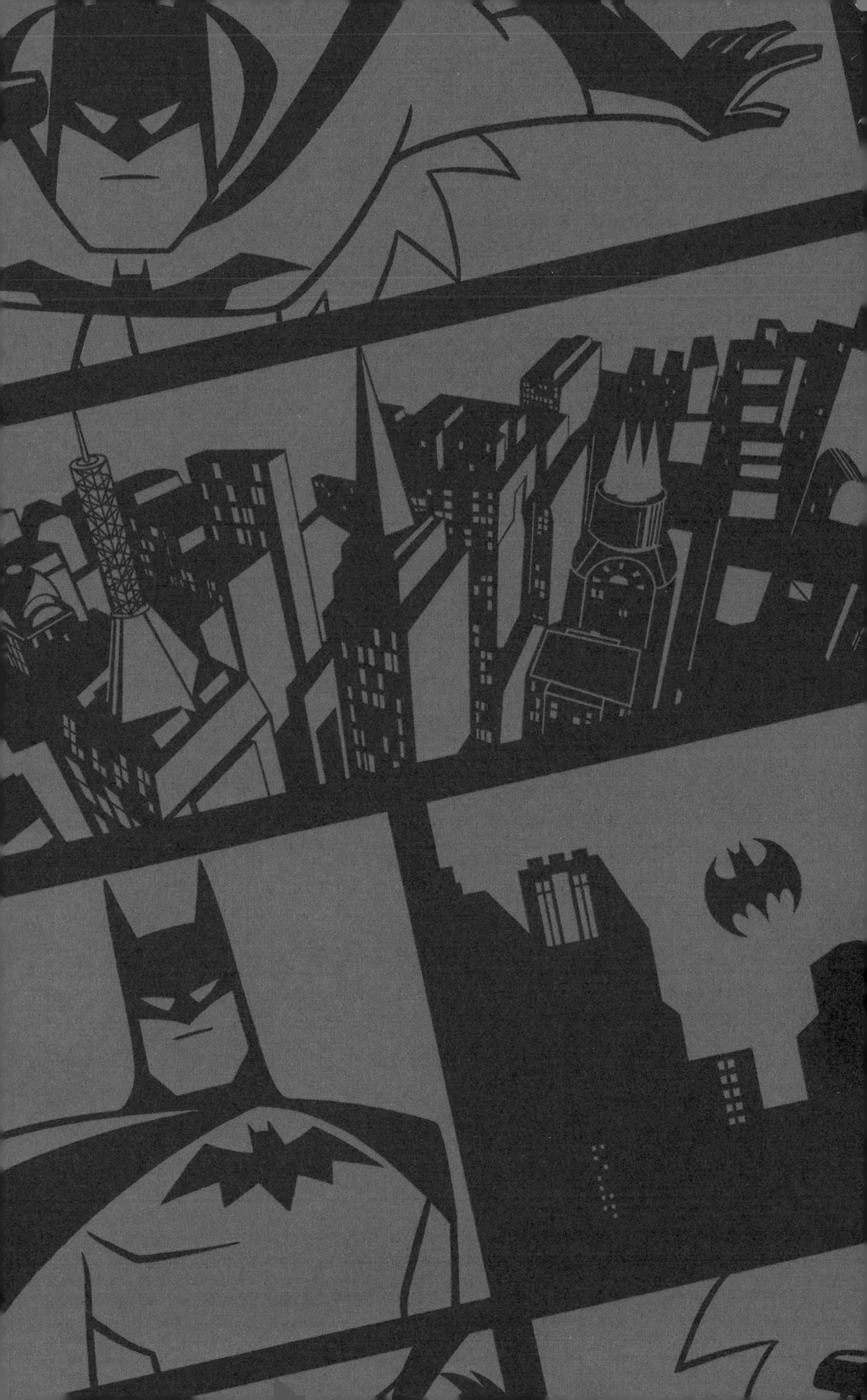

COMIC CHAPTER BOOKS

DC COMICS™ SUPER HEROES

BATMAN

STONE ARCH BOOKS

a capstone imprint

Batman: Comic Chapter Books are published by
Stone Arch Books,
A Capstone Imprint
1710 Roe Crest Drive
North Mankato, Minnesota 56003
www.capstoneyoungreaders.com

Star33544

Library of Congress Cataloging-in-Publication Data is
available on the Library of Congress website.

ISBN: 978-1-4342-9131-8 (library binding)

ISBN: 978-1-4342-9135-6 (paperback

ISBN: 978-1-4965-0097-7 (eBook)

Summary: Once again, Batman catches the Penguin in
the act, meaning more prison time for the villain. Since
the fowl felon has a bad habit of escaping his cell, the
Dark Knight delivers him to a privately run, impenetrable
prison this time around. But even from behind solid bars,
the Penguin finds a way to gain the upper hand... and
appoint himself warden! With all the thieves, thugs, and
crooks under his sway, the Penguin hatches a plan to
unleash his new army on Gotham City. The only shot
Batman has at preventing the Penguin's entire army
from flying free is to go inside the prison and battle the
bird-brained villain on his own turf...

Printed in the United States of America in Stevens Point, Wisconsin.
032014 008092WZF14

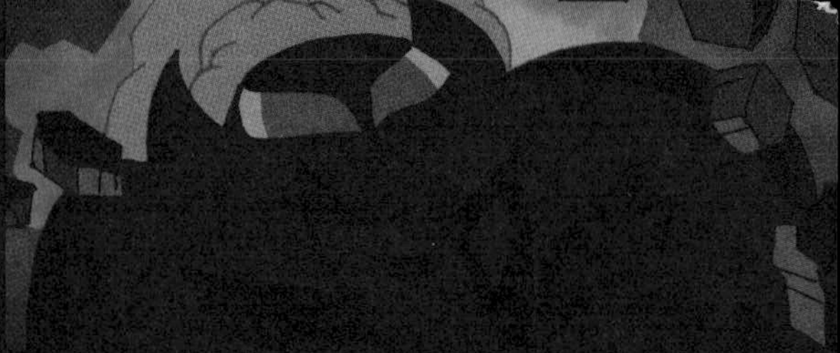

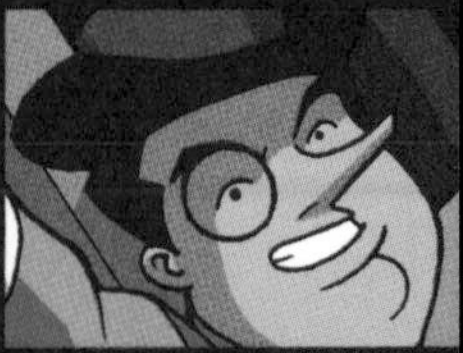

COMIC CHAPTER BOOKS

DC COMICS™ SUPER HEROES

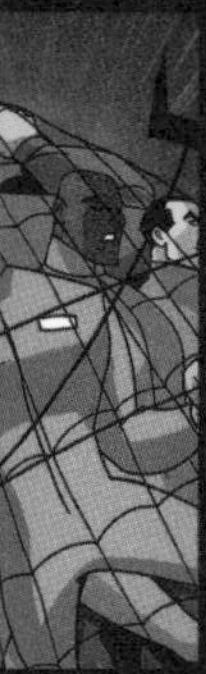

BATMAN™

PRISONER OF THE PENGUIN!

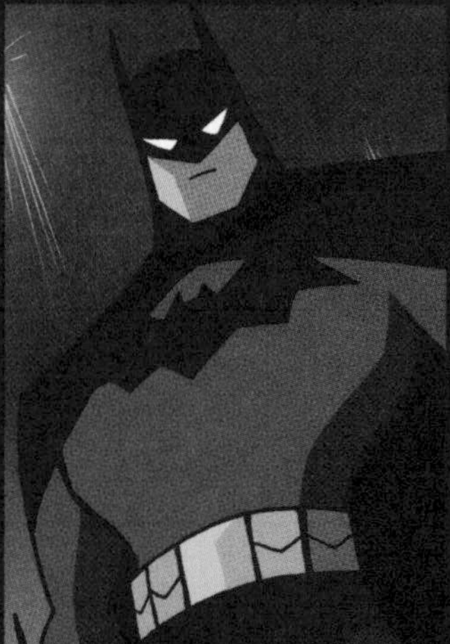

Batman created by Bob Kane

written by
Scott Sonneborn

illustrated by
Luciano Vecchio

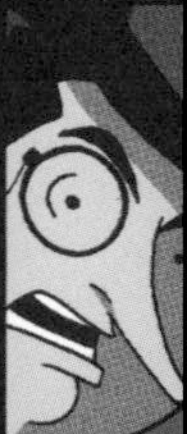

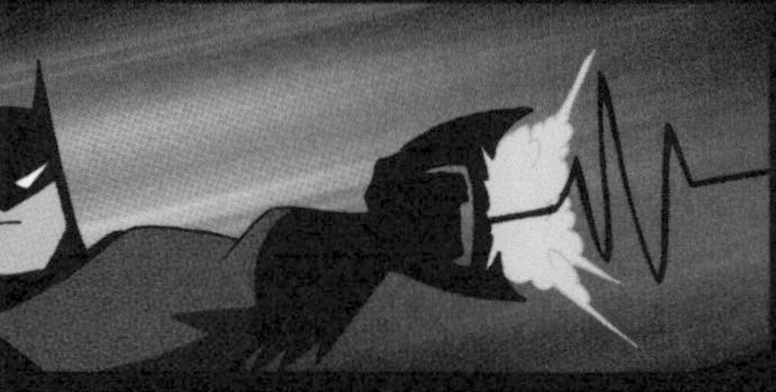

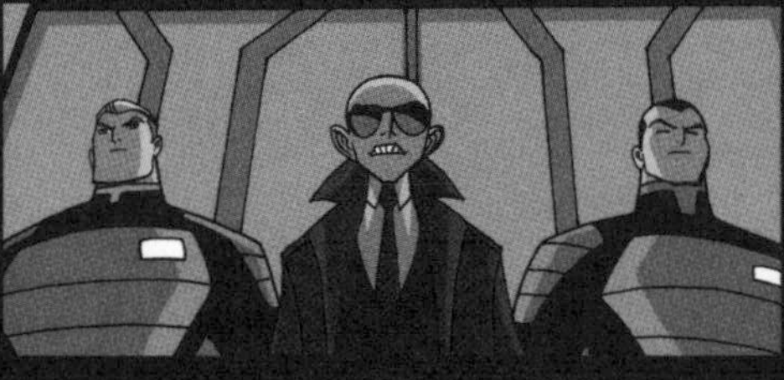

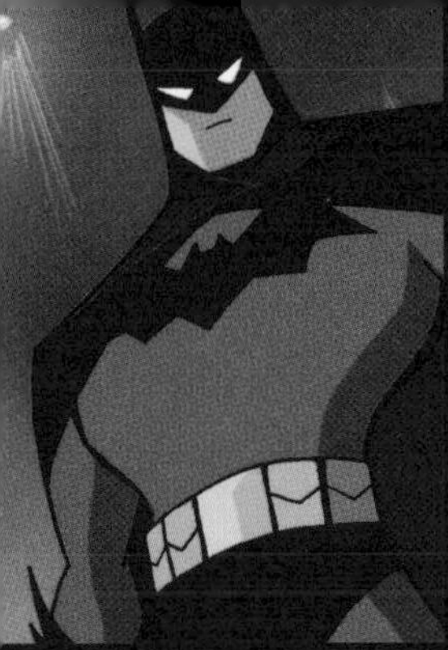

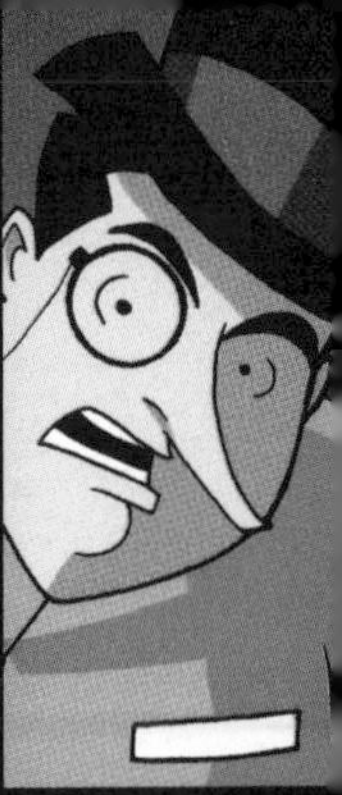

TABLE OF CONTENTS

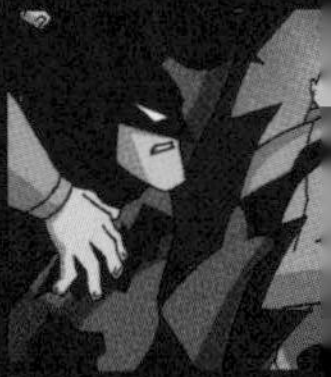

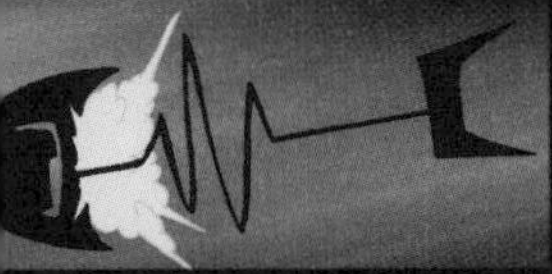

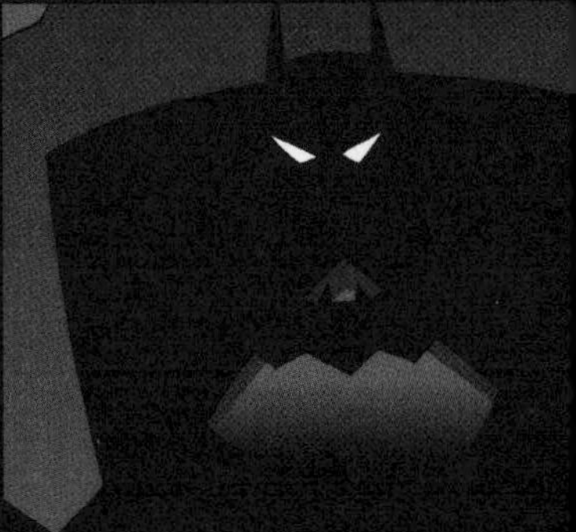

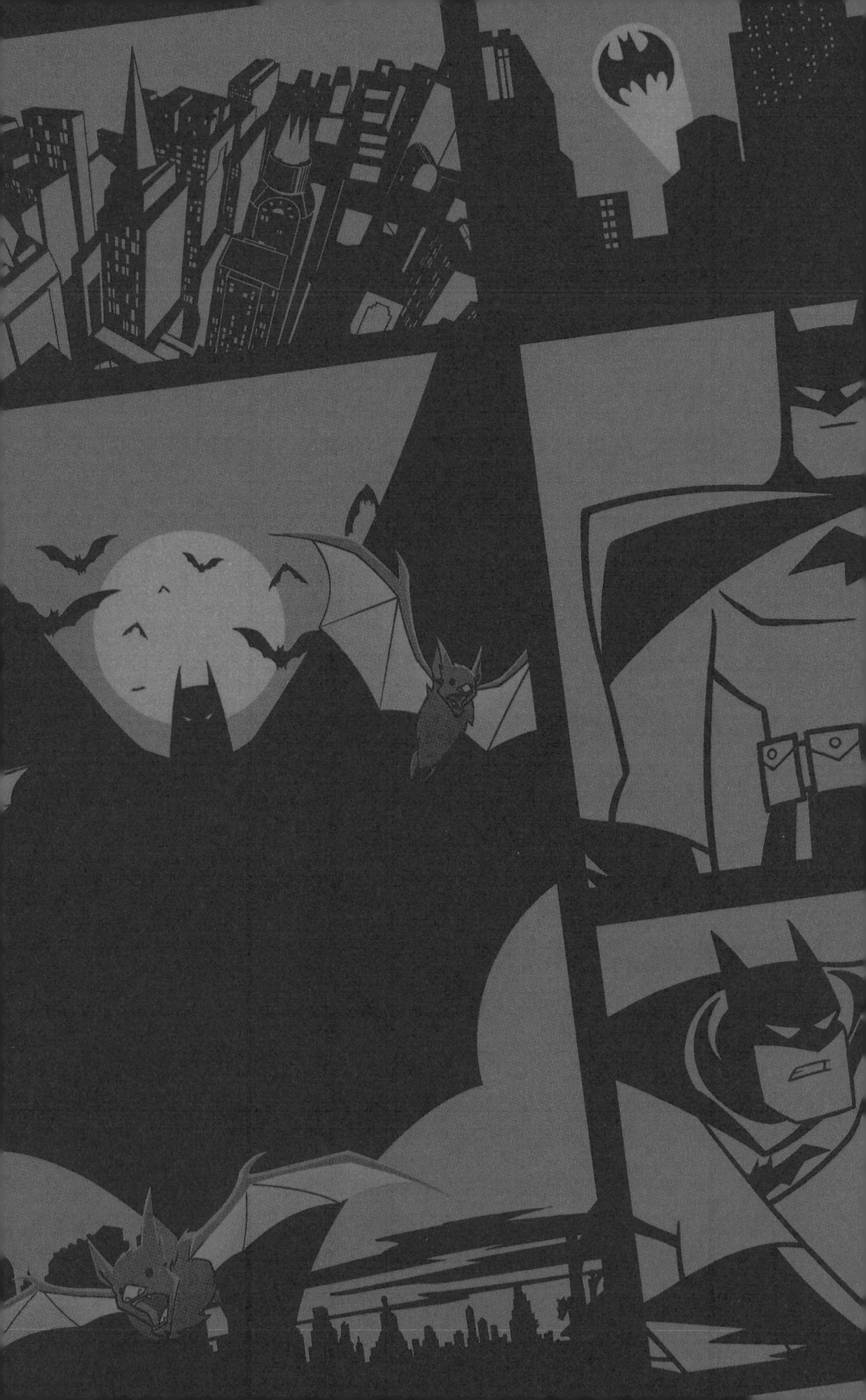

CHAPTER 1

THE CHASE!

CRUNCH!

CRUNCH!

CRUNCH!

The Batmobile's armored tires rumbled over the broken glass that littered the moonlit street.

The glass was from the window of The Gotham City Jewelry Exchange. A thief had smashed his way in. Now he was on his way out — along with a bag full of diamonds.

The thief leapt into a truck as the Batmobile roared up.

SCREEEEE!

The truck sped off. Batman shifted the Batmobile into high gear. The chase was on!

"Stop your vehicle!" Batman shouted through the Batmobile's loudspeakers.

The thief's only response was to pick up speed. His truck raced toward an intersection. A car was trying to cross — and the truck was going to hit it!

Batman activated the Batmobile's loudspeakers again. "Pull over!" he yelled.

The driver of the car yanked on her steering wheel. The truck flew past, missing her by mere inches.

Batman put his boot down on the gas pedal. As the Batmobile raced forward, the Dark Knight pushed a button.

CLICK!

SHHHOOOSH!

Wind rushed in as the Batmobile's roof slid open. Batman unbuckled his seatbelt and leapt out through the opening in the roof.

CLUNK!

He landed on the Batmobile's hood! He braced himself with both legs, riding on top of the Batmobile as it zoomed down the street.

Which meant there was no one inside the Batmobile to steer it. Up ahead was a sharp turn. If the Batmobile kept going straight, it was going to crash.

Balancing himself on the hood, the Dark Knight quickly reached into his Utility Belt. He took out a device the size and shape of a cell phone — the Batmobile's remote control.

Pushing buttons on the remote, Batman steered the Batmobile around the sharp corner and gained ground on the truck.

"Stop!" Batman shouted to the thief driving the truck. But he didn't stop.

Instead, the thief wildly swerved into the Batmobile!

CRUNCH!

The side of the truck slammed into the Batmobile's door. Batman slipped off the hood. But he was prepared for that to happen — he already had his grapnel gun out.

He fired it.

CRUNK!

The grappling hook sank into the back of the truck.

REEEEEEEEE!

The grapnel gun's cord retracted and instantly pulled Batman onto the truck.

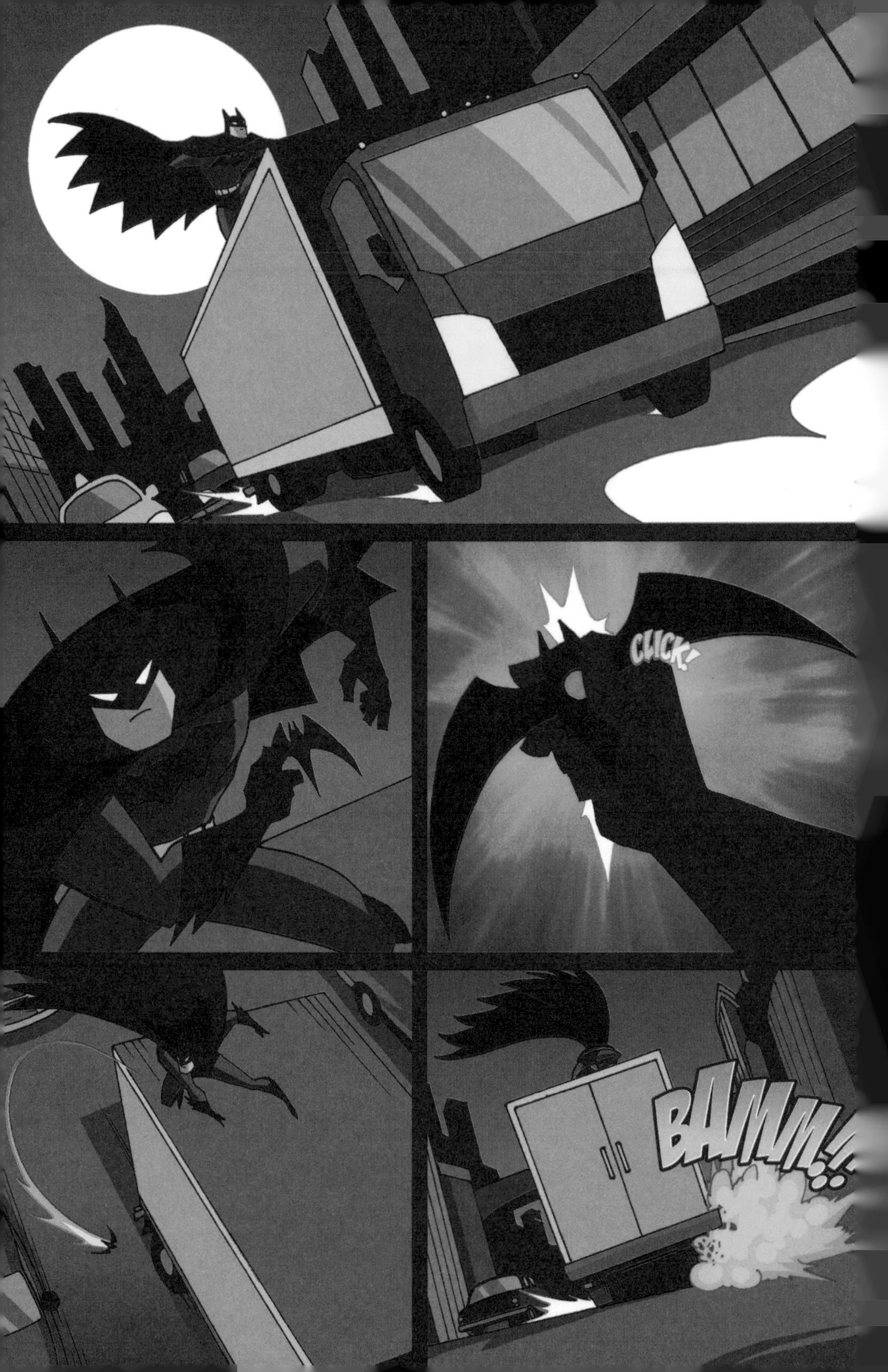
CLICK!
BAMM!!

The truck spun in a circle. Batman held on tight as the truck slammed into an empty building.

HISSSSSS!

Smoke gushed out of the crumpled engine as the truck stopped moving.

The Dark Knight grabbed the stunned thief and pulled him out of the truck. "You're the fourth thief I've caught tonight!" growled Batman. "The rest were following orders from the Penguin. Are you?"

The terrified thief nodded. Even though Batman had caught one of the Penguin's men, he wasn't happy.

Unfortunately, there was no way Batman could catch the Penguin. He'd already been caught two months ago by the Dark Knight. Since then, the Penguin had been in prison. So why were his men still running wild in Gotham City?

"Somehow, though, he's still organizing crimes from inside his cell," Batman said to himself. "And that has to stop."

* * *

An hour later, the Batmobile pulled up in front of the prison that held the Penguin. The massive stone building stood tall on the outer edge of Gotham City. Unlike Arkham Asylum or Blackgate Penitentiary, this prison was a private one owned by a businessman. Batman would not be welcomed here like he would be at those other prisons.

Batman parked the Batmobile and jumped out. He was met by two of the prison's guards.

"That's far enough," one of them barked.

"No one gets through the prison gate unless the Warden says so," said the other.

Just then, the massive prison gate rose. As it did, a man walked out from underneath it. Both guards saluted him. "Good evening, Warden," they said.

"At ease, men," said the Warden. Then he turned to face the Dark Knight. "What are you doing here, Batman?"

"I need access to your prison," Batman said.

The Warden thought for a moment. "I think it's better that you don't," he said. "If you were to enter my prison, it could cause a riot. After all, you're the reason most of the prisoners are in there."

"There's only one prisoner I'm interested in," said Batman. "The Penguin."

"Cobblepot?" replied the Warden. "He's been a model inmate! I run my prison by a strict set of rules. Strict but fair. If you're good, you get special privileges. If you break the rules once, you get kitchen duty. Break the rules twice, and you get sent to the hole."

The Warden smirked at Batman. "Cobblepot has earned every perk and never had kitchen duty once," said the Warden. "I only wish all my prisoners were like him."

"Very few crooks are like the Penguin," said Batman. "He's a criminal genius. Even now, he's using that genius to plot crimes. From inside your prison, right under your nose."

"If that's the case, then I will deal with it," the Warden said firmly. "As you say, it is my prison."

"Call Commissioner Gordon," Batman told the Warden. "He'll tell you I can be trusted."

"Yes, I've heard all about how Commissioner Gordon trusts you," said the Warden. "However, he has no authority here. This prison is owned by a private company. We have a contract with Gotham City to house their criminals, but we follow our own rules here."

Batman narrowed his eyes. *I can tell where this is heading,* he thought.

"One of those rules is that no one is admitted without my permission," continued the Warden. "Now, if you will excuse me, I need to return to my work."

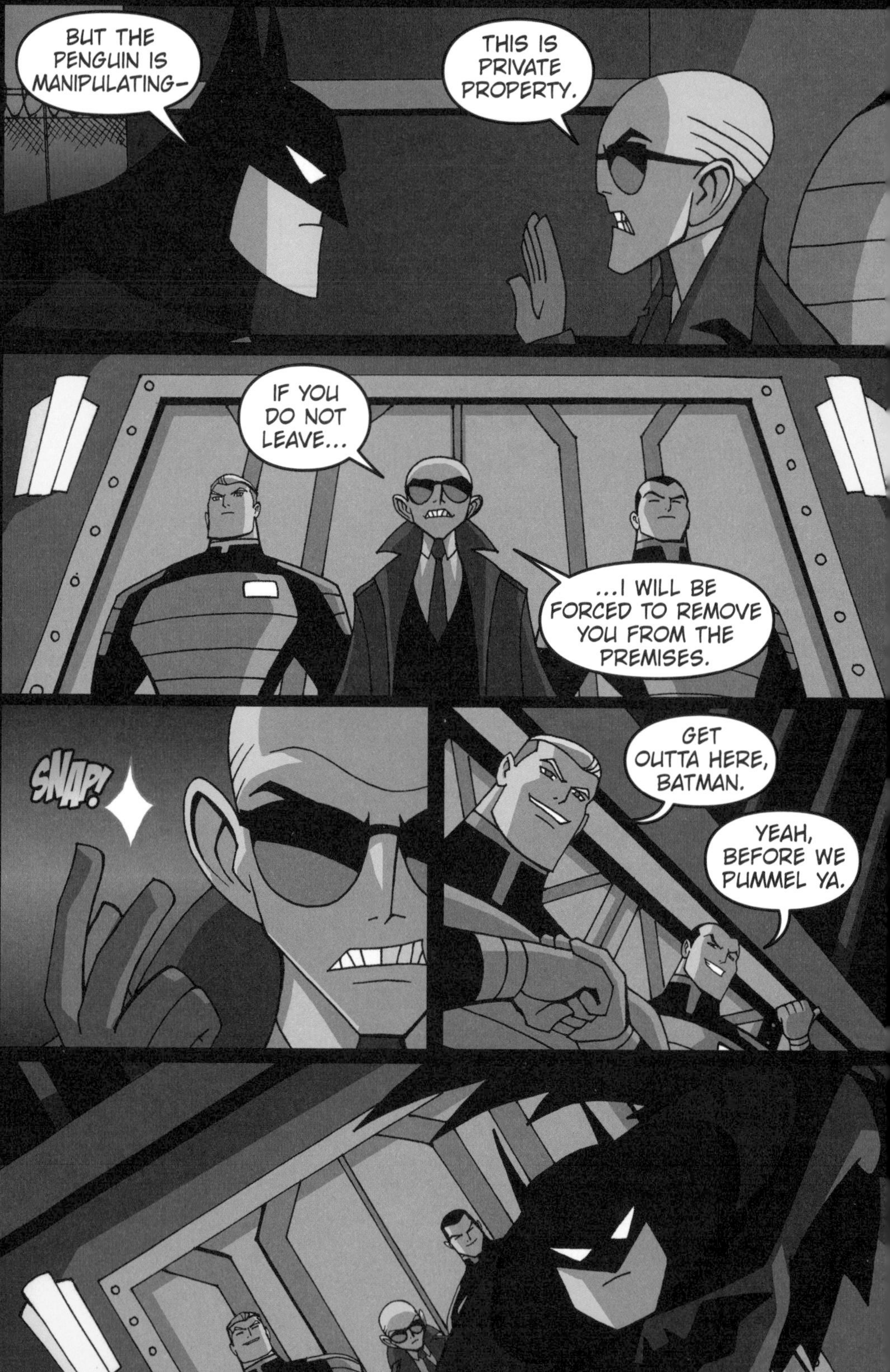
BUT THE PENGUIN IS MANIPULATING-
THIS IS PRIVATE PROPERTY.
IF YOU DO NOT LEAVE...
...I WILL BE FORCED TO REMOVE YOU FROM THE PREMISES.
SNAP!
GET OUTTA HERE, BATMAN.
YEAH, BEFORE WE PUMMEL YA.

Batman didn't want a fight and had no other options. So he turned and climbed back into the Batmobile and left for the Batcave.

* * *

A half hour later, the Batmobile squealed into the Batcave. It was still moving as Batman leapt out. He used his remote control to slow the car to a stop as he hurried to the Batcomputer.

TAP

TAP

TAP!

Batman's fingers danced over the keyboard as he quickly searched for everything he could find about the prison. If the Warden wouldn't let him inside, he had to find another way to find out what the Penguin was up to.

The Batcomputer pulled up the prison's floor plan. Batman studied it on his supercomputer's giant screen. It was just as he had guessed when he was outside the prison: It was solidly built. The only way in or out was through the heavy-duty front gate.

And there was no way the Warden would open the gate for Batman. He had made that clear enough.

Then Batman realized something. "Maybe there is a way I can get the Warden to open the gate for me."

The Warden said the prison was owned by a private company, Bruce thought. *Well, what if Bruce Wayne bought that company?*

Though few people knew it, Bruce Wayne was Batman. A billionaire, Bruce had more than enough money to buy any company he pleased, including the prison the Penguin was housed in. And once he did, he could order the Warden to let Batman in.

To buy the company, though, Batman had to figure out who owned it.

TAP

TAP

TAP!

His fingers tapped across his keyboard.

Batman was able to track down the prison's subcontractors, which were the companies that supplied the prison's food and did its laundry. He hoped to track their transactions back to the prison's owner.

However, after another hour of searching, Batman still couldn't find the name of the person who owned the prison.

"That's strange," Batman said. "That information should be in the public records. That means whoever owns the prison doesn't want people to know who he or she is. It could be a fake corporation, or a group of investors. It could take weeks to determine. And I don't have that kind of time."

Batman rubbed his chin through his cowl. "I can't buy the prison if I don't know who to buy it from," Batman said. "So how can I get the Warden to open the gate and just invite me inside?"

Suddenly, Batman thought up a potential solution. It was risky. Very risky.

But it was also the only way Batman could get inside the prison. And he had to do so in order to find out what the Penguin was doing, or his behind-bars crime spree would tear apart Gotham City.

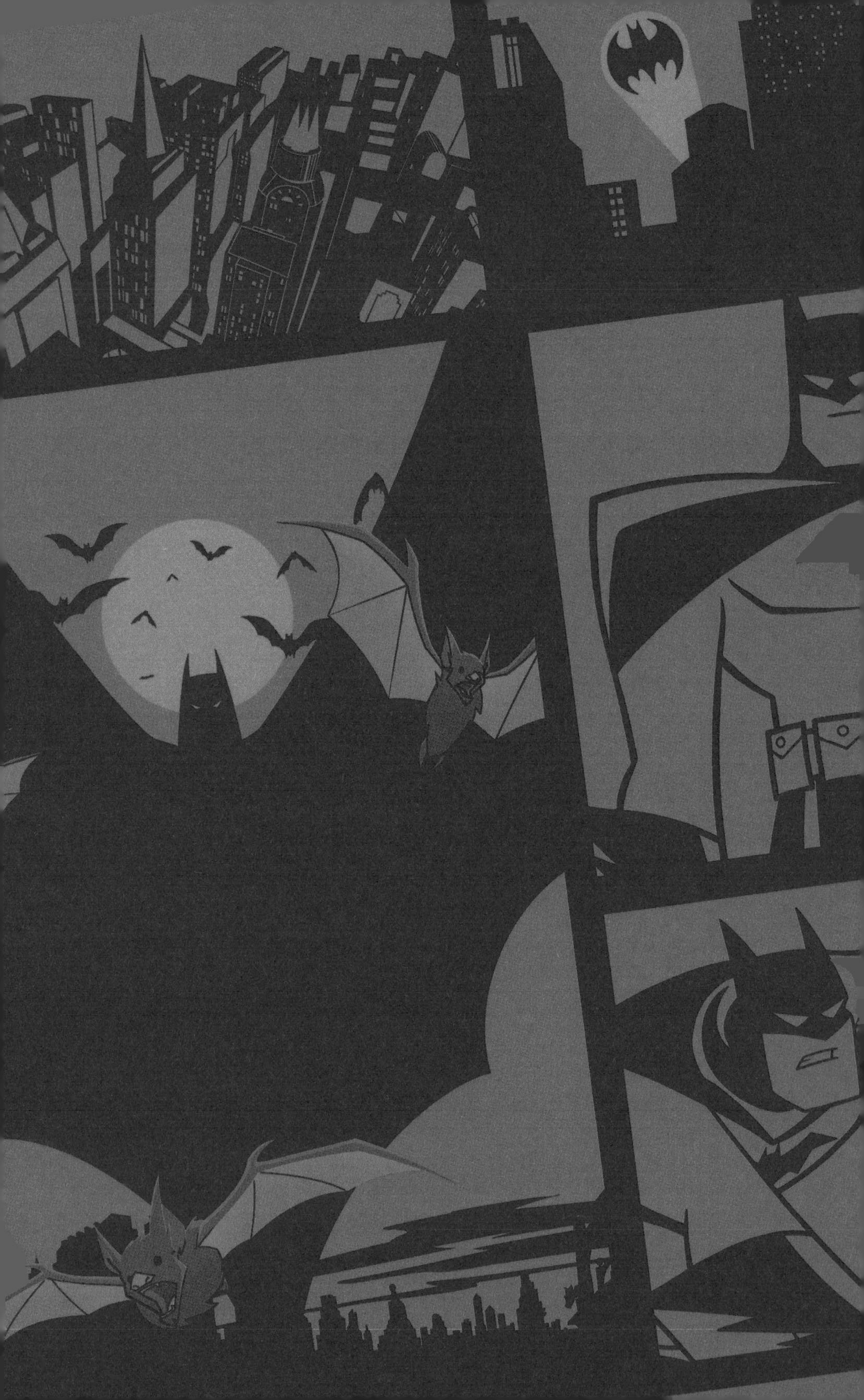

CHAPTER 2

PRISONER!

Two days later, the Batmobile screeched to a stopped in front of Gotham City's Police Headquarters.

Commissioner Gordon and a dozen police officers poured down the steps toward the Batmobile.

"Dropping off more crooks for us to put in jail?" asked Commissioner Gordon.

"Just one," Batman announced over the Batmobile's loudspeakers.

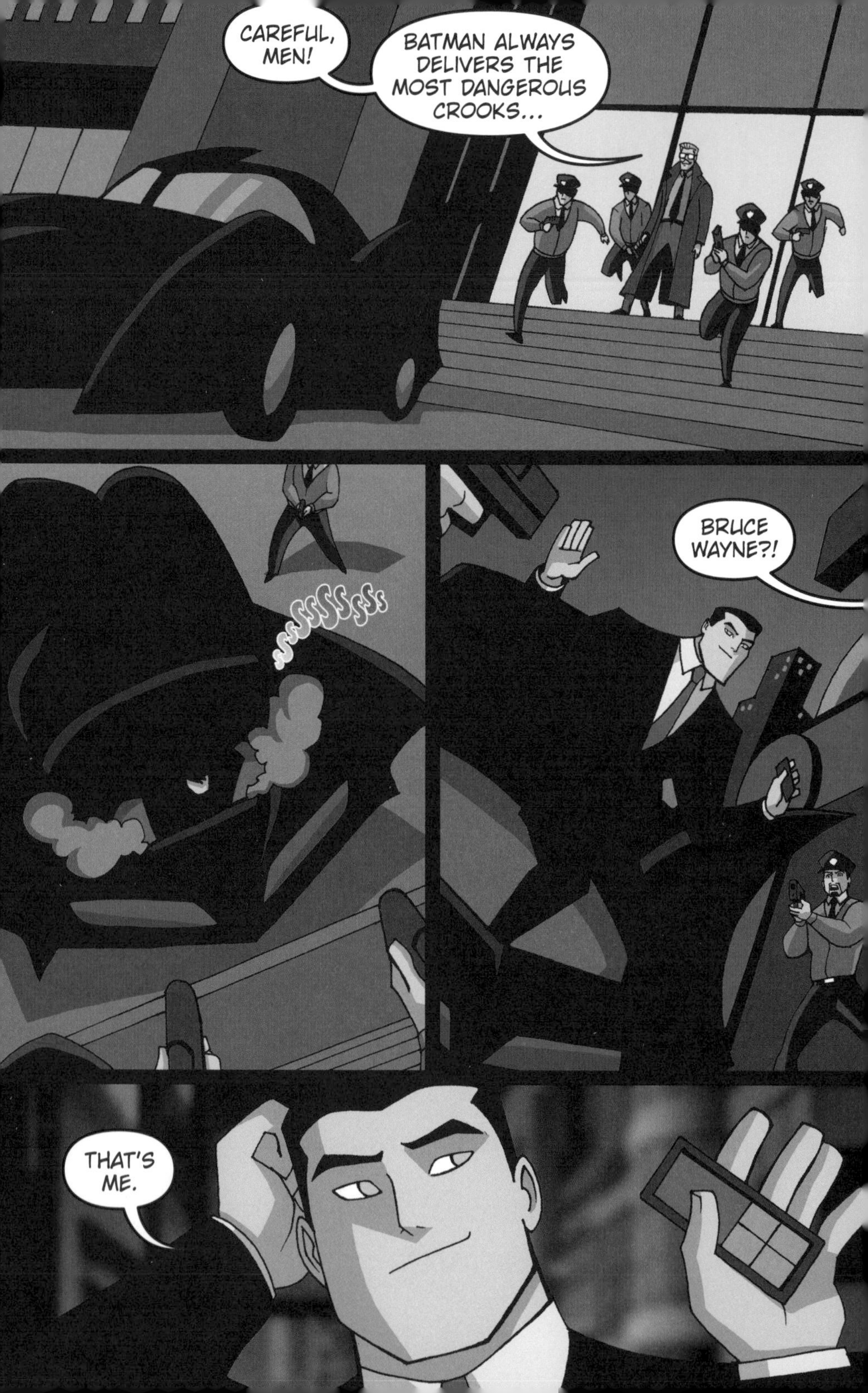
CAREFUL, MEN!
BATMAN ALWAYS DELIVERS THE MOST DANGEROUS CROOKS...
SSSSSSSSS
BRUCE WAYNE?!
THAT'S ME.

CRUNK!

The Batmobile's door slammed closed.

SCHROOOOM!

The Batmobile raced off.

Bruce was secretly driving the Batmobile with the remote control hidden in his hand. He steered it around the corner, then pushed a button that sent the Batmobile to a pre-programmed location.

"Stop!" ordered a police officer.

"What?" Bruce asked.

The officer saw that Bruce had something in his hand. "What's that?" the policeman asked. "What are you hiding in your hand?"

"It's my phone," Bruce said, which was true since it also functioned as a cell phone. "Since I'm under arrest, I thought I should call my attorney."

Bruce knew, though, that if anyone looked too closely at the device, they would discover its other purpose. Which is why Bruce dropped it and then pretended to trip over it.

CRUNCH!

The remote was crushed to pieces under his shoe. "That was clumsy," said Bruce. "I suppose I'm nervous. I've never been arrested."

Commissioner Gordon slapped a pair of handcuffs on Bruce. "You have now," he said.

"But-but this is Bruce Wayne!" exclaimed one of the police officers. "He's a millionaire!"

"Try billionaire," Commissioner Gordon said. "But I trust Batman. Mr. Wayne, assuming the charges add up, you are going to prison."

* * *

An hour later, Bruce Wayne was standing outside the prison as its gates opened.

The Warden appeared. "Mr. Wayne," he said. "I'm sorry to meet you under these circumstances. But all the same, welcome. I'd tell you to enjoy your stay, but that probably won't happen."

Bruce gulped, playing the part of the fretful billionaire. *Well, I got the Warden to open the gates for me,* Bruce thought as he marched inside. *Now comes the tricky part.*

As soon as he was inside, Bruce was told to change into his prison uniform. The Warden took Bruce's $4,000.00 suit and $400.00 tie, as well as his wallet and everything in his pockets.

Bruce had known he was going to have to hand over anything he brought with him, which is why hadn't brought his Batman costume, his Utility Belt, or any of his special gear.

Bruce took a deep breath, then entered the cellblock as a prisoner. Even though he was wearing the prison uniform, he felt exposed. Vulnerable.

The inmates howled from their cells as Bruce walked past them. Bruce recognized many of their faces. As Batman, he had put them there. The men in the cells were thieves, kidnappers, and worse.

Although Bruce understood the psychology of the criminal mind, they were still dangerous and unpredictable.

SWUNK!

SWUNK!

SWUNK!

All of their cell doors suddenly swung open! Hundreds of criminals walked out of their cells. Without any of his gear, there was nothing Bruce could do against so many enemies if they attacked him.

But none of them did. "Yard time!" shouted one of the guards. "Get out there. All of you! Move!"

Bruce let out a sigh of relief as the prisoners obeyed the guard's order and marched out to the yard.

"That includes you, smart guy!" the guard said to Bruce.

Bruce shrugged and did as he was ordered. He left the cellblock and entered the prison yard.

Out on the prison yard, Bruce saw the prisoners had arranged themselves in several groups. He noticed a few of the groups as thugs and hired hands for various villains Batman had faced.

Birds of a feather flock together, he thought. *How fitting.*

Bruce did a quick count in his head. Each group was comprised of about 40 prisoners and led by a single guard. To Bruce, the guards looked like sergeants, leading soon-to-be soldiers through basic training. They did pushups, jumping jacks, and drills just like soldiers in the army.

Bruce's thoughts were interrupted when a guard shoved him in the back. "Get moving like the others!" he ordered.

Bruce knew he had to act like a snob. If he didn't, the guard might start to get suspicious. He had to continue playing the part of billionaire Bruce Wayne.

"I'm afraid they didn't teach this sort of thing at my boarding school," Bruce said. "Maybe you should demonstrate the exercises to me first?"

"You will not talk back to your commanding officer!" someone said behind Bruce.

Bruce turned to find himself face to face with the Warden.

"You're no longer a member of high society," the Warden said as he walked up to face Bruce. "Now you're a member of *my* society. You're *my* prisoner, just like all the rest."

The Warden stuck his finger in Bruce's face. "They obey my orders and do the drills," he said. "And so will you."

Bruce scanned the yard. Not all the prisoners were doing the drills.

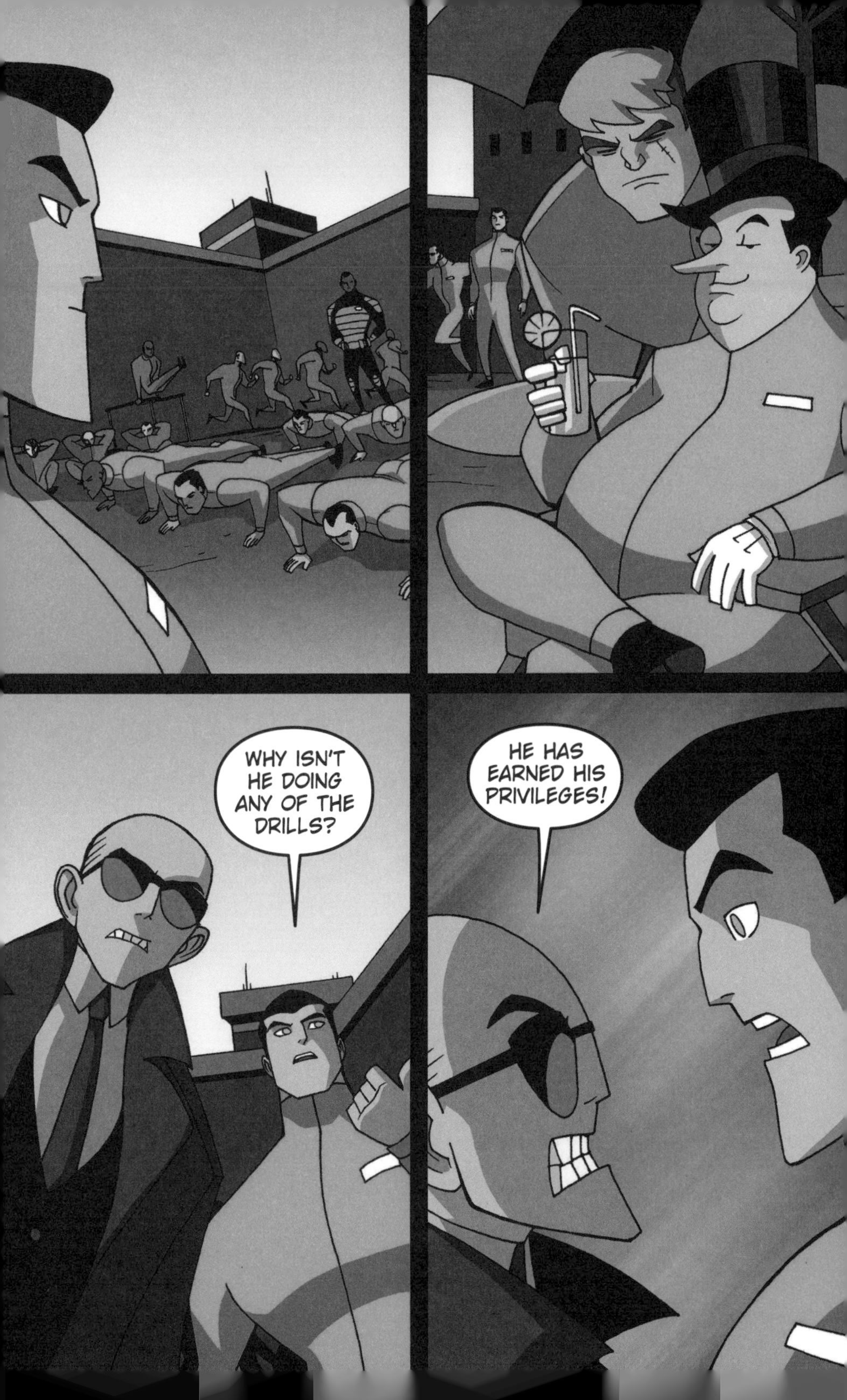
WHY ISN'T HE DOING ANY OF THE DRILLS?
HE HAS EARNED HIS PRIVILEGES!

"You're new here," the Warden added. "So you haven't earned anything here yet. You can earn privileges, or you can earn punishments. The choice is completely up to you. Now fall in line and get to work like the rest of the prisoners. Drop and give me twenty!"

"How about I just stand here and give you a twenty?" said Bruce. "You took my wallet with my clothes, but if you go and get it, you'll see that it is filled with twenties. Fifties and hundreds, too."

The Warden looked surprised and annoyed. "It seems as though you need to be taught a lesson," he said.

"Begin combat training!" the warden yelled. Immediately, all over the yard, the inmates began to practice martial arts.

Why are prisoners learning combat skills in prison? Bruce wondered.

The Warden waved a prisoner over. "Sir, yes, sir!" the prisoner said, saluting. The man was twice as big as Bruce.

"I want you to give Mr. Wayne here a martial arts lesson," the Warden told the huge prisoner.

WHUMP!

The warden shoved Bruce toward the thug. "And make sure the lesson is painful," the Warden added. "Very painful."

As Batman, Bruce had studied martial arts for years. He was one of the best in the world. But Bruce couldn't let anyone know that.

Bruce had two choice. The first one was to take the beating. He didn't much like the idea of some thug wailing on him, though.

The second option was to continue playing the fool. Most everyone expected Bruce Wayne to be stuck-up, spoiled, and slightly bumbling when it came to physical tasks.

Bruce didn't feel like taking a punch, so he decided on the second choice. *This is going to be tricky,* he thought.

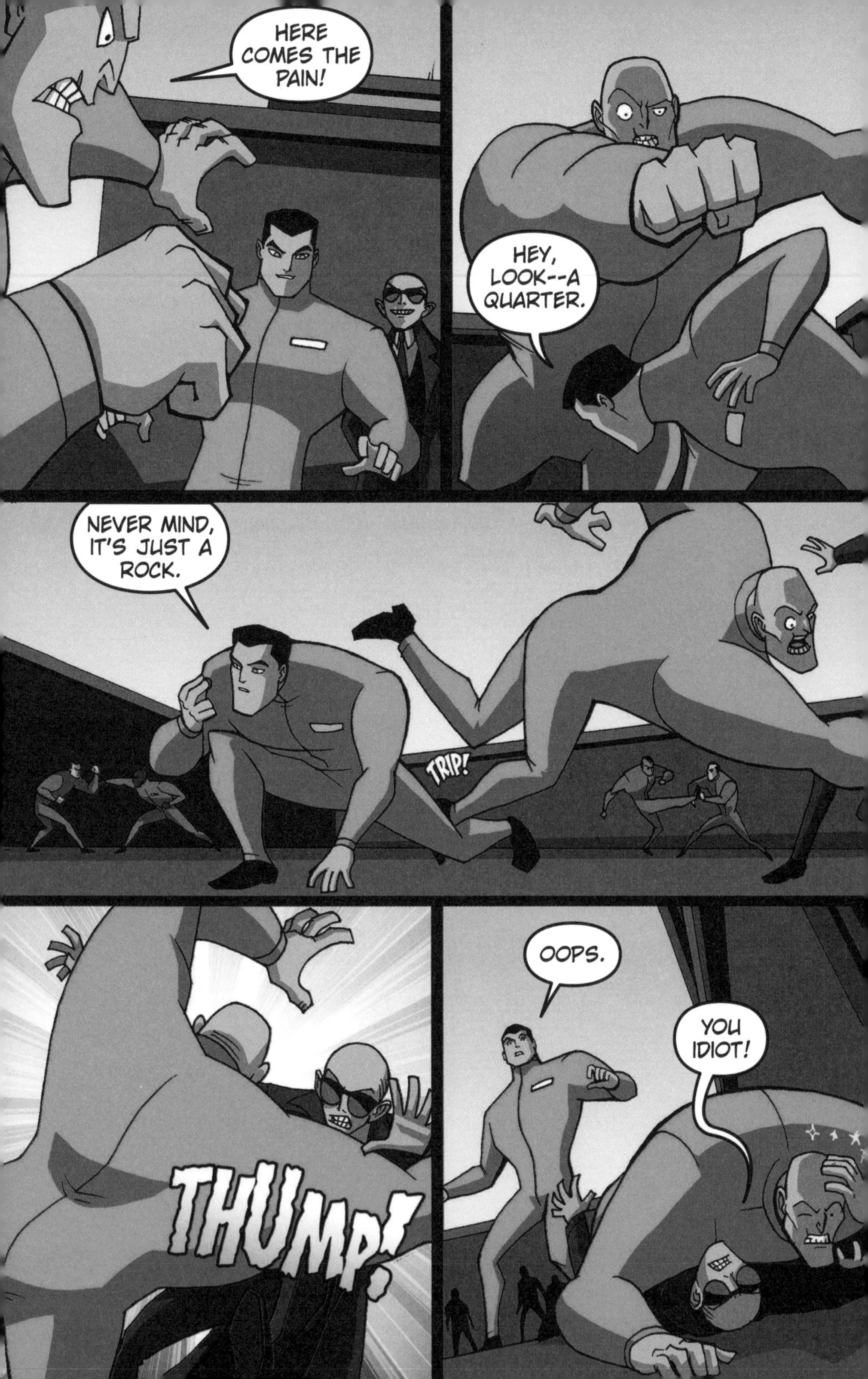
HERE COMES THE PAIN!
HEY, LOOK--A QUARTER.
NEVER MIND, IT'S JUST A ROCK.
TRIP!
THUMP!
OOPS.
YOU IDIOT!

Bruce had succeeded — the whole thing had looked like an accident!

Bruce rubbed the back of his head, trying to look embarrassed. "Sorry about that," Bruce said, a smile on his face. "It was a complete accident."

The Warden didn't smile back. "It's against the rules for any prisoner to lay a hand on the Warden!" he growled. "Even by accident!"

Bruce opened his mouth to speak, but thought better of it. It wouldn't help his cause to point out that he hadn't actually touched the Warden. People like him didn't enjoy it when others pointed out their mistakes, and Bruce didn't want to get in any more trouble than he already had.

One of the guards rushed over to help the Warden get back to his feet. "What should we do with him?" the guard asked.

The Warden brushed himself off. "It's his first offense," he said. "You know what that means. Put him on kitchen duty."

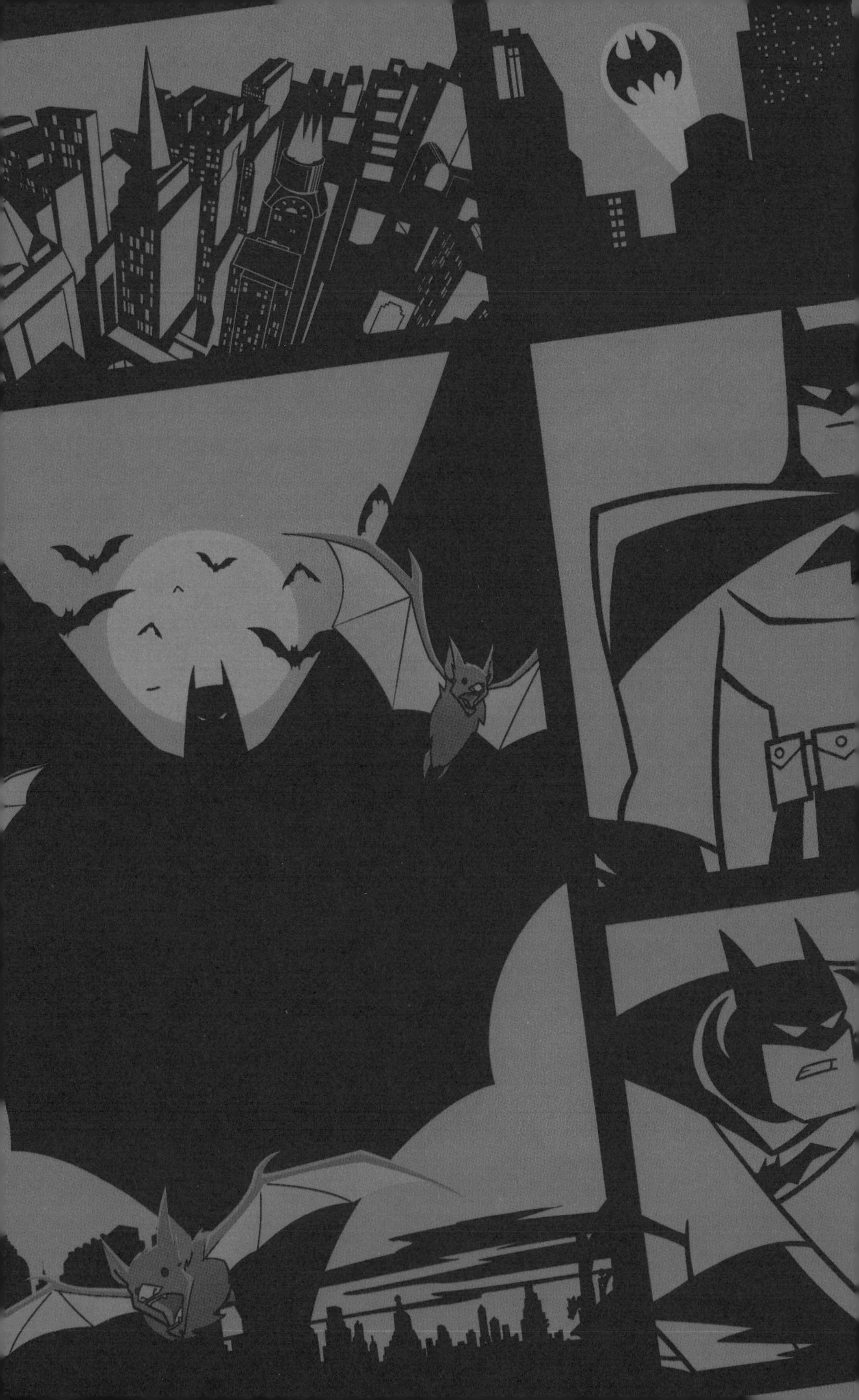

CHAPTER 3
PUNISHMENT!

Ten minutes later, the guard shoved Bruce inside the kitchen. "Get to work!" he ordered.

"Work?" asked Bruce. "My dear boy, I've never worked a day in my life. I don't know the first thing about working in a kitchen."

"Well, here's the first thing," said the guard, as he shoved Bruce again. "Go inside the storeroom and get more oatmeal!"

Bruce did as he was told and went to the storeroom. Once inside, he quickly shut the door behind him. He rushed past the oatmeal to a giant vat of powdered eggs. It was as big as a mailbox.

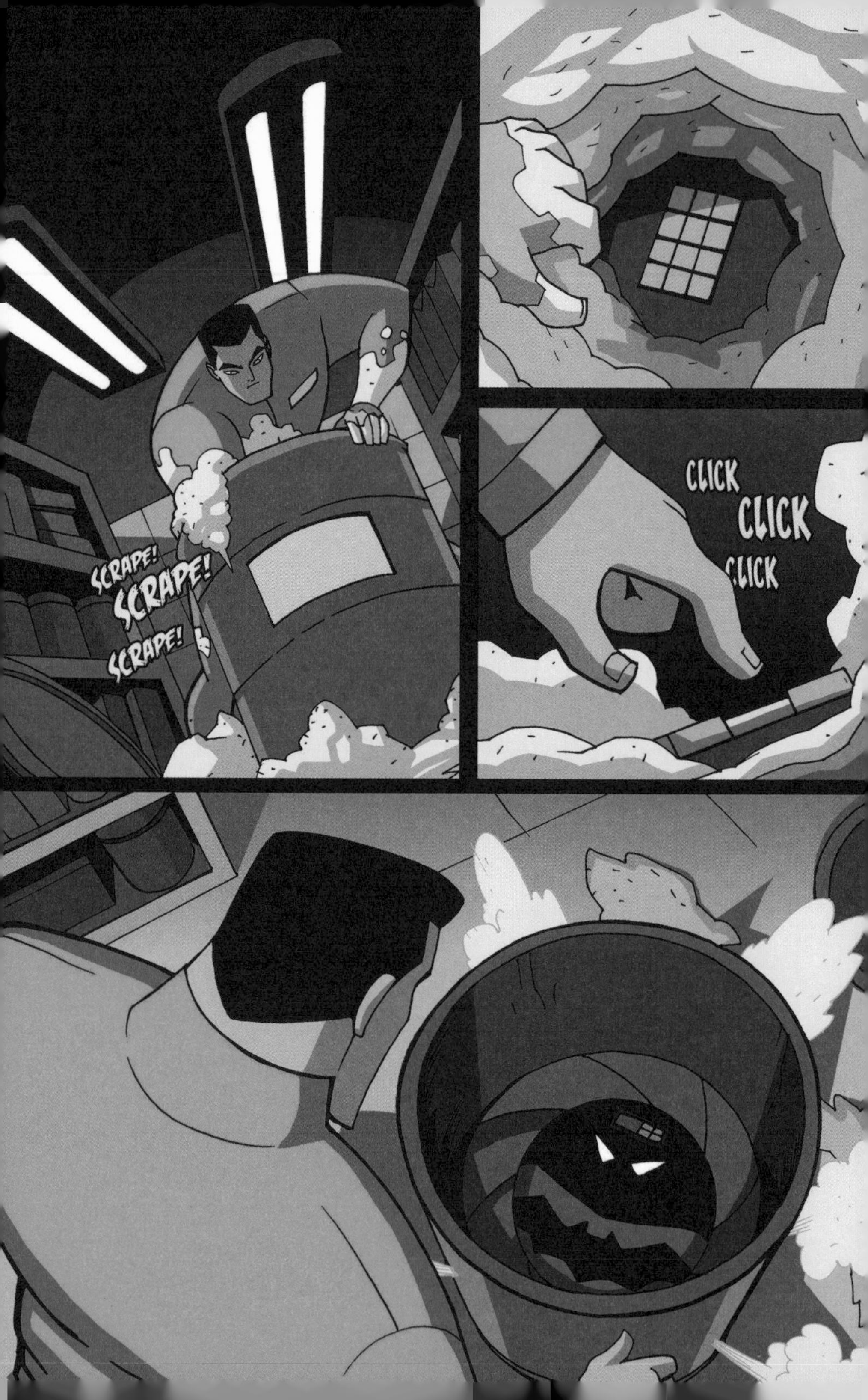
SCRAPE!
SCRAPE!
SCRAPE!
CLICK
CLICK
CLICK

A day earlier, Bruce had purchased the subcontractor that supplied the prison's food. Once he owned that company, he was easily able to hide his equipment in one of their daily deliveries.

The secret compartment in the container of powdered eggs only had enough space to hold his costume and the spare Batmobile remote. His Utility Belt was hidden in a nearby container of dried beans.

The night Batman had first met the Warden outside the prison, the Warden had told him that the first punishment prisoners were given was kitchen duty.

"Looks like getting in trouble on the yard worked," Bruce said to himself.

Bruce quickly concealed his Batman costume and the Batmobile's remote control beneath his prison uniform. Then he raced over to the metal vat of beans. He was about to reach inside, when . . .

WHAM!

The storeroom door slammed open and a hulking inmate marched in.

"Boss wants to see you," the thug snarled.

"Why would the Warden want to see me now?" asked Bruce. He shifted his uniform to make sure his costume and the Batmobile remote couldn't be seen underneath it. "The Warden just sent me here."

"No," snarled the inmate. "Not the Warden. I said the *boss* wants to see you. You don't know anything, do you?"

Bruce hesitated. The thug wasn't bright, but he couldn't think of a reason to stall.

"C'mon, you better get moving!" the inmate ordered, cracking his knuckles.

Behind the inmate, the door to the kitchen was open. Bruce saw a dozen more prisoners hard at work there.

If I dig out my bean-covered weapons right now, Bruce thought grimly, *those prisoners are sure to see me and find out that I'm Batman. I have to wait for the right moment.*

The big inmate was getting more and more impatient. "C'mon!" he growled.

Bruce had no choice.

Bruce shrugged and followed the inmate, leaving his weapons and tools hidden in the bean vat.

The hulking inmate led Bruce through the cellblock. They passed row after row of prison cells, most of which were occupied by inmates.

Then they climbed the metal steps up to the second level. Most of these cells were empty, though.

They walked past more empty cells until they came to the last one. This cell was not empty, and it was different from all the rest.

The inmate pushed Bruce toward the cell from behind. "Move," he said.

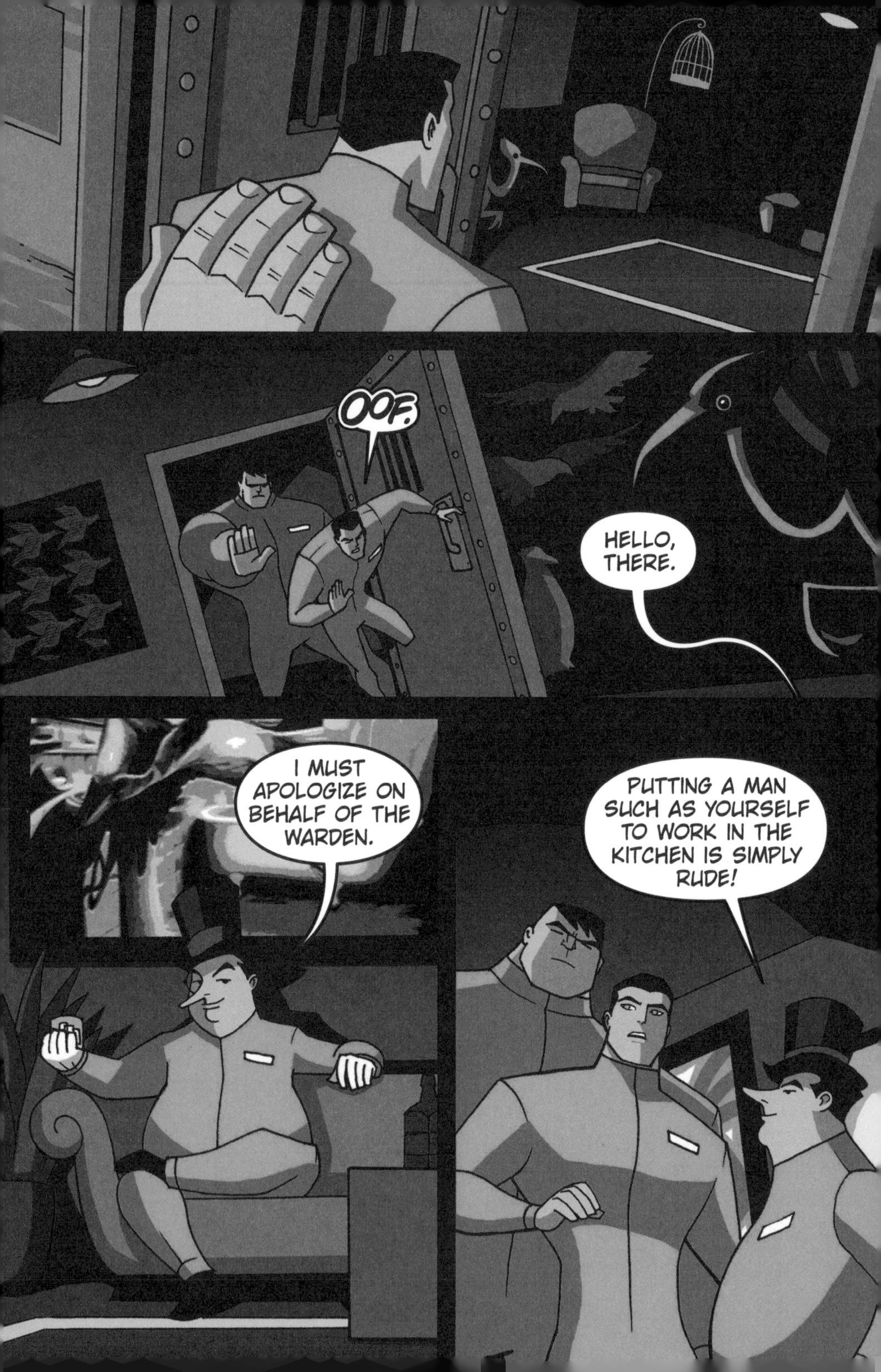
OOF.
HELLO, THERE.
I MUST APOLOGIZE ON BEHALF OF THE WARDEN.
PUTTING A MAN SUCH AS YOURSELF TO WORK IN THE KITCHEN IS SIMPLY RUDE!

Bruce shrugged. "I guess when you're a prisoner, you have to get used to taking orders from the Warden," he said.

The Penguin took a sip of the ice-cold drink in his hand. "Yes," he said. "You would think that, wouldn't you?"

The Penguin waddled to his feet. "I didn't invite you here to talk about the Warden, though," he continued. "At least, not exactly. I've gotten to know all of the other prisoners very well since I've been here. But you are brand new. I have to decide if I can trust you."

He leaned in close to Bruce. "Because," the Penguin whispered, "I'm planning something big. Something very big."

"And what is that?" Bruce whispered. He couldn't believe his luck. This was exactly what he had come to the prison to find out!

The Penguin didn't answer. Instead, he shook his head. "I've already gone out on a limb telling you as much as I have," said the villain. "So first, you tell me. Can I trust you?"

Bruce was one of the smartest people in Gotham City. He knew he had to choose his words carefully.

Bruce nodded. "Of course," he said. "I didn't find success in business by breaking my promises."

Bruce knew that his word wouldn't be enough to gain the villain's trust. Sure enough, the Penguin shook his head again.

"Maybe you're telling the truth," the Penguin said. "Or maybe you'd tell the Warden everything I just told you. Only one way to know for sure."

The Penguin snapped his fingers.

"Yes, sir?" someone called.

Bruce turned to see the Warden enter the cell!

"You called, Mr. Cobblepot?" said the Warden. "Anything I can do for you, sir?"

"Yes," replied the Penguin. "You can listen to Mr. Wayne here. I think he has something he wants to tell you about my plans."

"Go right ahead, Mr. Wayne," the Warden said pleasantly. "If Mr. Cobblepot wants me to listen to you, I am more than happy to. He is the boss after all!"

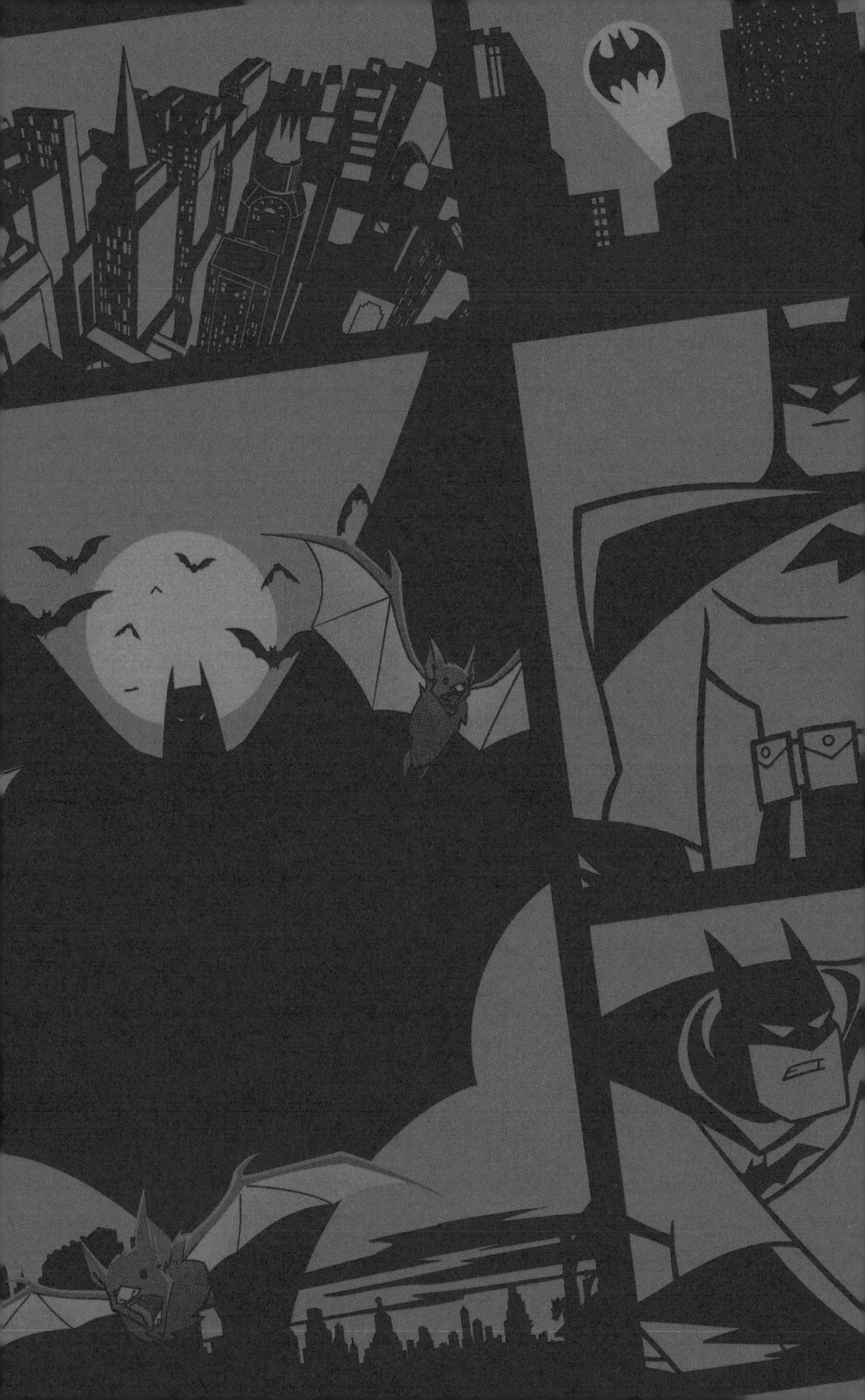

CHAPTER 4

THE PENGUIN'S PLAN!

Suddenly, Bruce understood. It all made sense. "You own this prison, don't you?" he said to the Penguin. "The Warden, the guards — they all work for you!"

The Penguin smiled. "Not just them," he said. "The inmates serve me as well. I've been training them, you see. I've turned them into a criminal army!"

"Why would you tell me all this?" Bruce asked.

"Because I have to be sure I can trust you, Wayne," replied the Penguin.

The Penguin walked around Bruce in a circle, as if observing him like a bird in a cage. "Tonight, I am going to unleash the criminal army I've been training on Gotham City," The Penguin said. "Batman has always been able to stop one or two of my men, but even the Dark Knight won't be able to stop an entire army of well-trained thugs!"

The Penguin stopped circling and stuck his beak right in Bruce's face. "See, these men have been trained to act like soldiers and obey my every command," the Penguin gloated. "Success depends upon their obedience. So you can see why I just have to know if the newest inmate in this prison would willingly go along with my plan."

Bruce nodded. "I won't interfere," he said. "I want to get out of this dump just as much as you do."

The Penguin frowned.

"I'd like to believe you, Mr. Wayne," the Penguin said. "I really would. Your assets would be a lot of help in the latter stages of plan to take over Gotham City. Unfortunately, I just can't risk trusting you."

"So what should we do with him, sir?" asked the Warden.

"This prison has rules," replied the Penguin. "Follow them. This prisoner has already been given kitchen duty. What is the next punishment he should receive?"

The Warden sneered. He gestured to his guards. "Send him to the hole!" he ordered.

* * *

The hole was what everyone in the prison called solitary confinement. It was a tiny cell just big enough to hold one prisoner. There were no windows or even bars. Just rough concrete walls and a solid steel door.

Bruce sat alone in the dark. He couldn't see out, and no light came into his cell.

However, there was one good thing about the darkness: no one could see Bruce in here!

Bruce slipped out of his prison uniform into his Batman costume that had been hidden under his uniform along with the Batmobile remote control.

That was all he had, though. His crime-fighting weapons and Utility Belt were still hidden in the vat of beans in the kitchen storeroom.

If he had even one of his explosive Batarangs, he could have easily blasted his way through the cell door. His laser torch would have cut through the concrete walls like butter. But he had neither of those things.

What he did have, though, was the spare Batmobile remote. *But what good is that?* Batman thought.

* * *

Inside the prison's front hall, the Penguin stood in front of his troops.

Before him were all the prison's guards and inmates. Each of the guards served as a sergeant, with a platoon of inmates standing at attention behind him. They looked every inch a trained army.

"All your training is about to pay off," the Penguin told his army. "And I do mean *pay*! Under my leadership and that of my second-in-command, the Warden, this criminal army will ransack Gotham City and steal every valuable item the city has to offer!"

The inmates all saluted. "Yes, sir!" they shouted in unison.

"You have been well trained," said the Penguin. "As long as you follow my orders, you will not fail. Instead, you will prosper. Each of you will be rich beyond your wildest dreams!"

As the men cheered him, the Penguin waddled toward the button that opened the massive front gate. "Gotham City will be ours for the taking!"

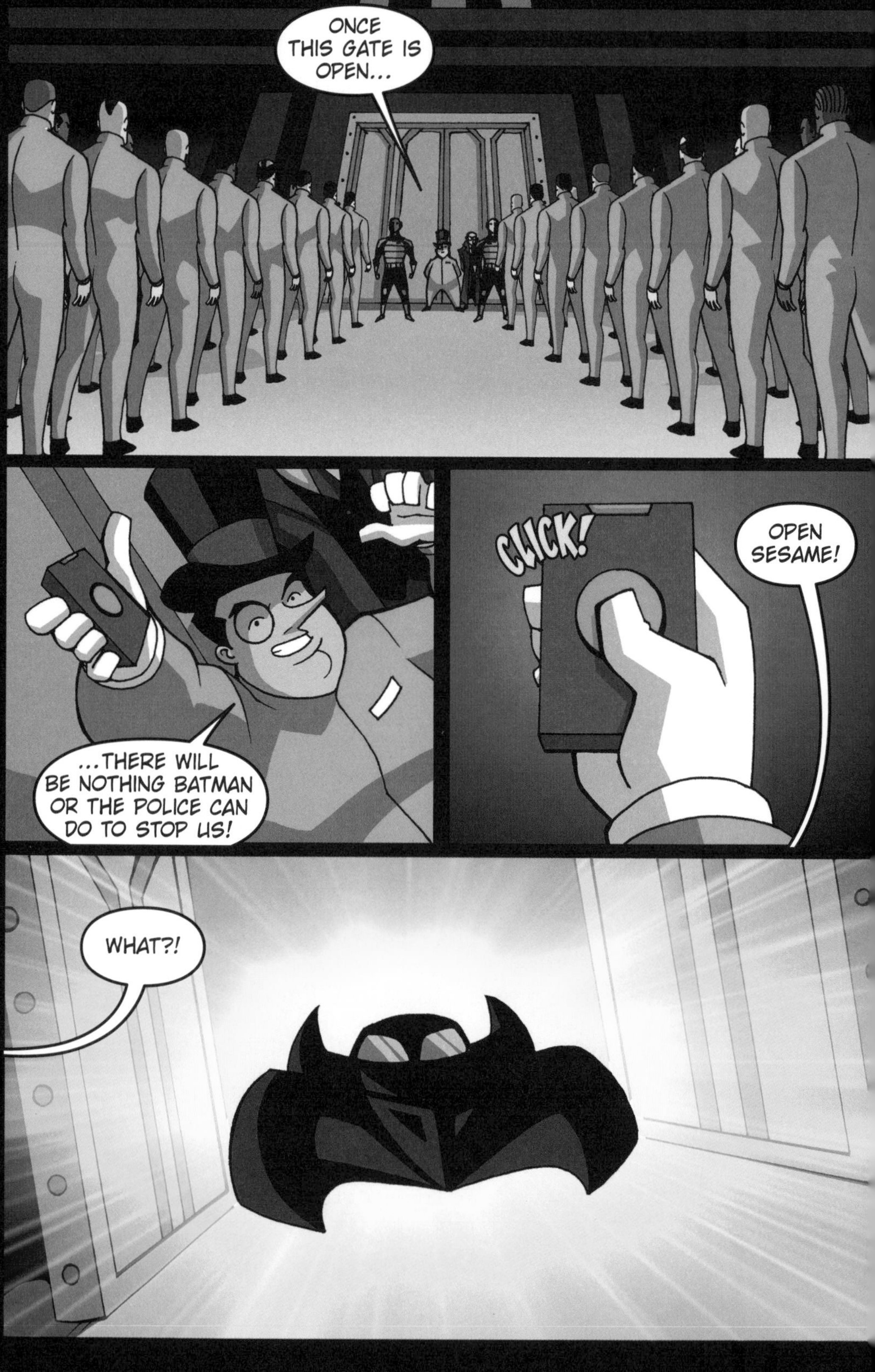
ONCE THIS GATE IS OPEN...
...THERE WILL BE NOTHING BATMAN OR THE POLICE CAN DO TO STOP US!
CLICK!
OPEN SESAME!
WHAT?!

That was all the Penguin managed to say as the Batmobile zoomed toward him. He jumped aside as the Batmobile slammed against the prison gate's control panel, shattering it.

WHA-THUNK!

The massive gate slammed shut, trapping the Penguin and his army of criminals inside the prison! The Batmobile raced deeper into the prison.

The Penguin leapt to his feet and turned to face his criminal army. "Squad A, stop Batman!" he ordered. "The rest of you men, stay here! We have to get this gate open!"

"Yes, sir!" shouted the prisoners and the guards.

The inmates in Squad A were only too happy to chase down the Batmobile. After all, Batman was the reason most of them had been locked up in the first place. They saw it as their best and only chance for revenge.

But meanwhile, in his dark cell in solitary confinement, Batman sat still. His fingers were the only things that moved. They tapped on the Batmobile's remote control as he used it to drive the Batmobile through the prison!

He was thankful for the darkness because he had to completely focus in order to remember every detail of the prison's floor plan he had seen on the Batcomputer. While Batman was smarter than almost anyone else in Gotham City, this task was pushing his brain to the limit. He had to remember every hallway and corner in the prison's floor plan. At the same time, he had to calculate the Batmobile's exact speed to know when to turn.

If he failed, then the Batmobile would never reach his cell!

SCREEEEEEEEEEEE!

Batman heard the Batmobile squeal down the halls and through the cell halls. It turned sharply.

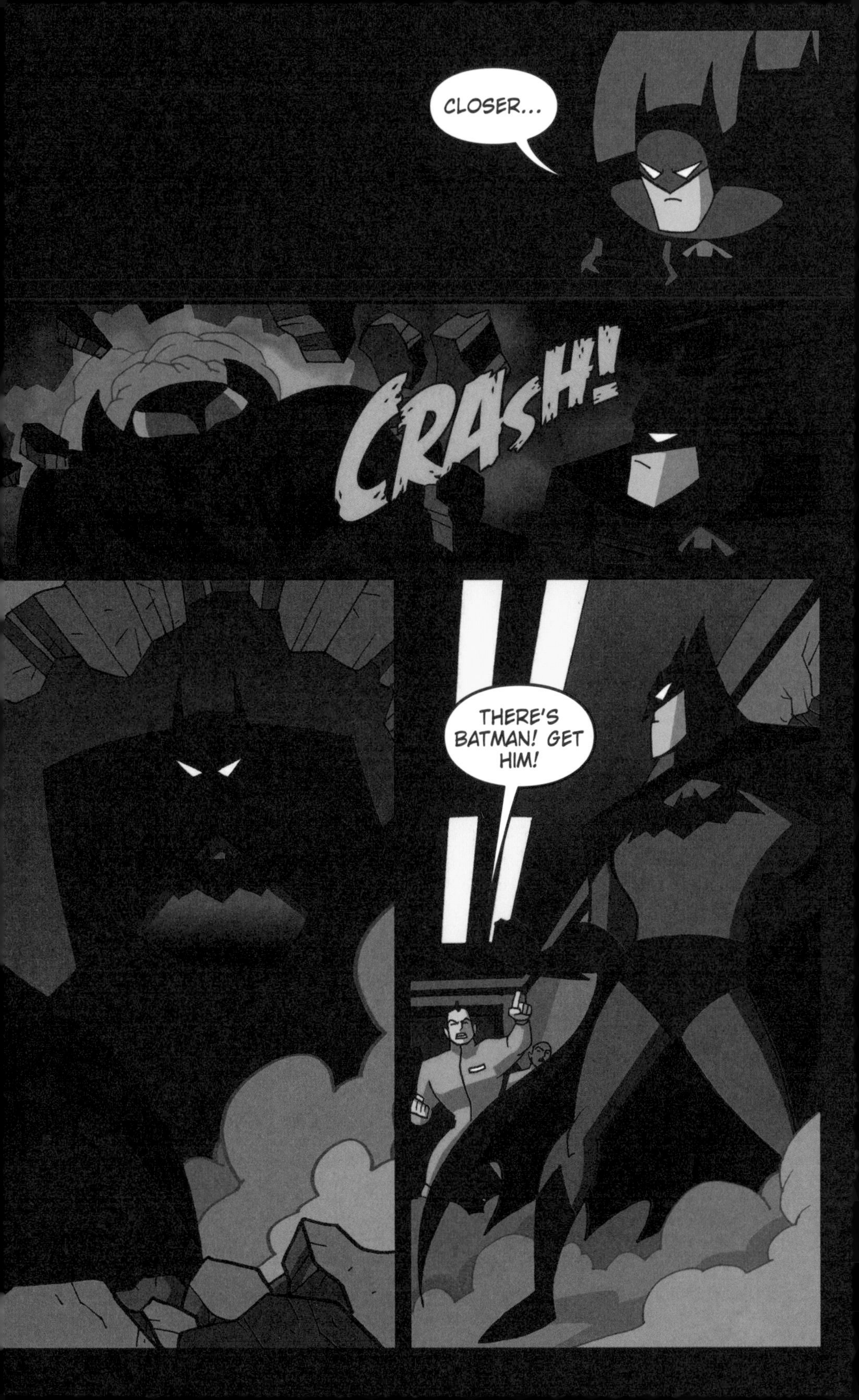
CLOSER...
CRASH!
THERE'S BATMAN! GET HIM!

Batman was surrounded.

One of the many thugs pointed at him. "Get him!" he yelled. "Don't let him get away."

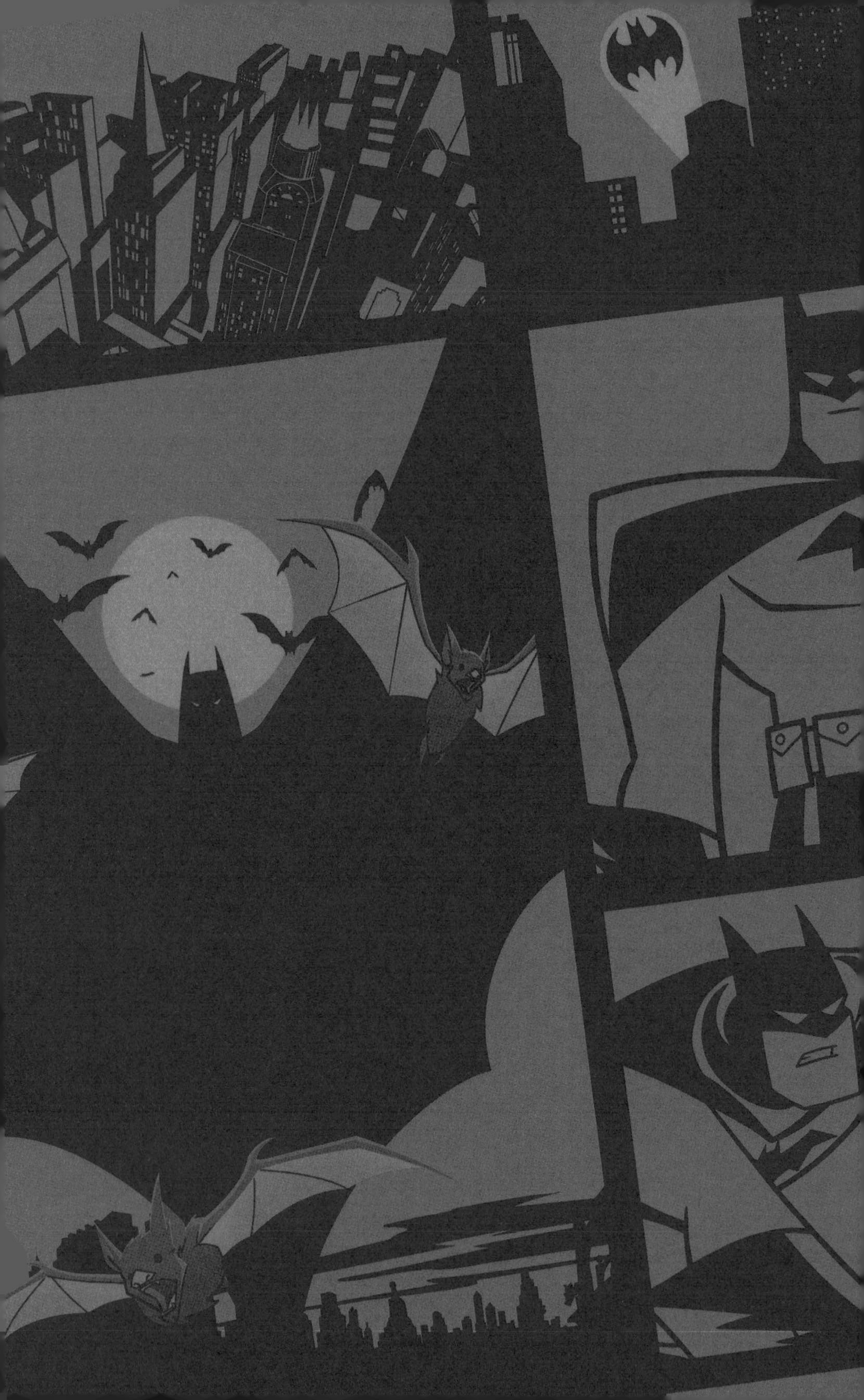

CHAPTER 5

PRISON BREAK!

The squad of criminals circled Batman. Their nostrils flared with anger. Their fists were clenched and held up near their chins.

The Dark Knight braced himself as the forty inmates of Squad A charged at him.

WHAM!

Batman knocked out the guard leading them. But the prisoners kept coming.

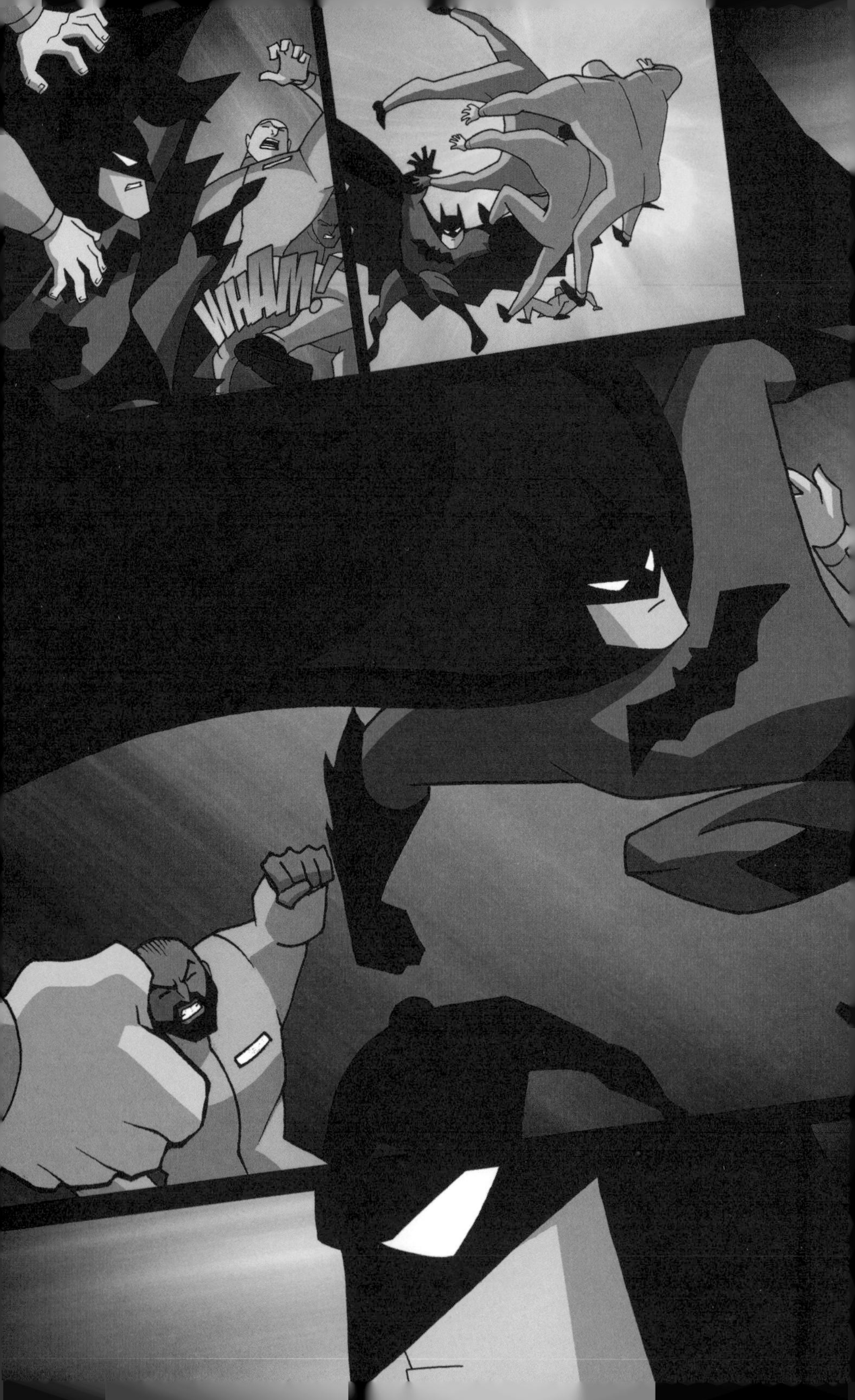
WHAM!

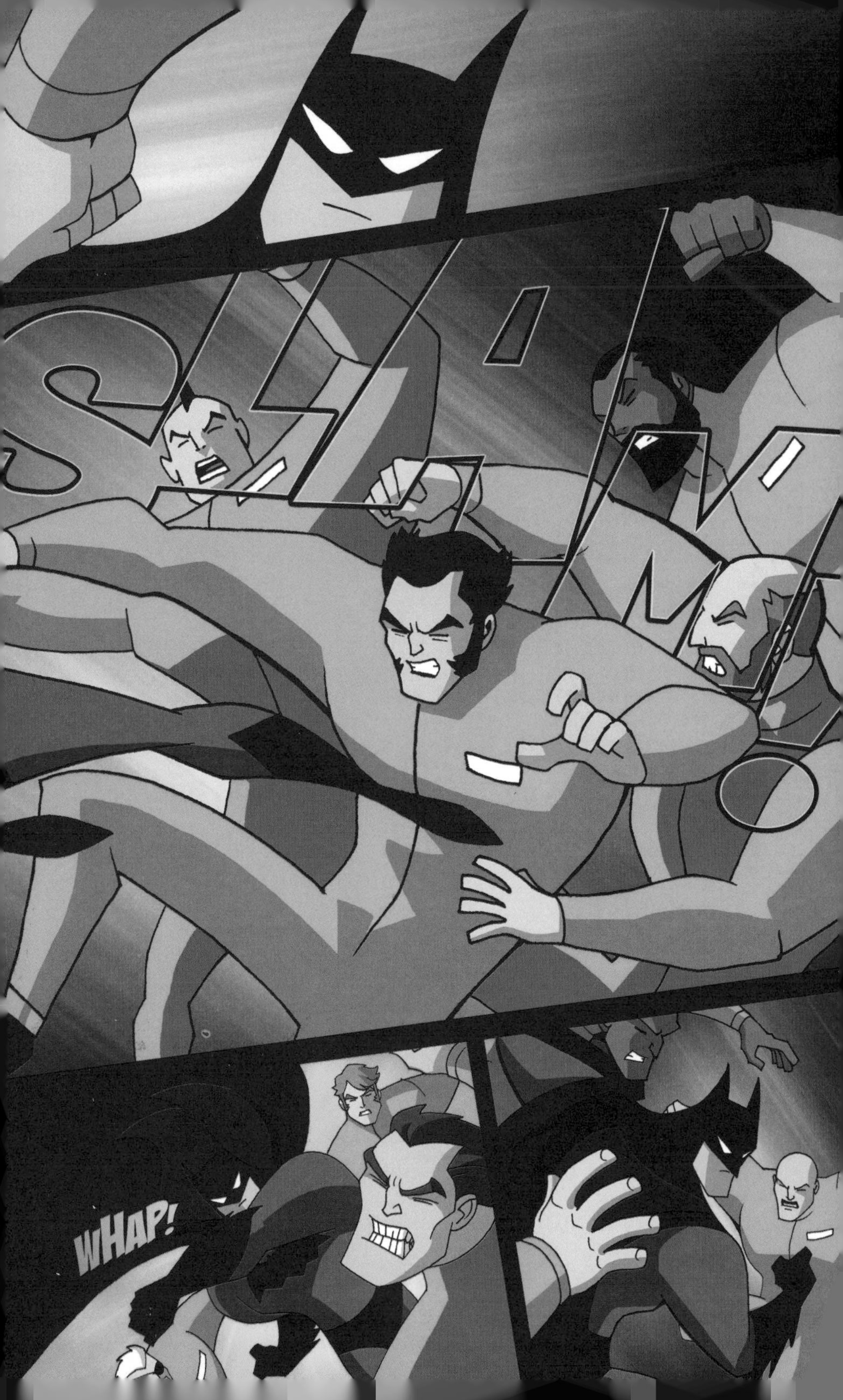
SLAM!
WHAP!

Batman fought them two, three, or four at a time. He twisted and dodged and kicked and punched. But for every one he knocked down, two more lunged at him.

There were just too many. Batman pushed a button on the Batmobile's remote. Nothing happened. The Batmobile was wrecked. Neither it nor the remote control worked.

As the prisoners surrounded him, Batman looked around desperately for something he could use against them. Unfortunately, prisons usually take special care not to leave anything lying around that can be used as a weapon. This prison was no different. All Batman had were his fists and his feet.

And his head!

BAM!

Batman head-butted the prisoner charging at him. Even as he did, Batman was using his head in a second way. He was strategizing, calculating his next move.

He had to get to the front gate. As many prisoners as there were here, ten times more were waiting to get out and run wild through Gotham City.

Unfortunately, there were still thirty prisoners from Squad A blocking his way. So Batman ran in the other direction. As the criminals of Squad A chased him, Batman ran farther and farther away from the front gate.

The prisoners chased him into the kitchen, which was exactly where Batman wanted to go!

BAMP!

SSCHLUNK!

Batman opened the lid. The strong smell of refried beans escaped the giant vat. Batman ignored it as he reached down through the beans.

CLICK

CLICK

CLICK!

He punched in a secret code that opened the vat's false bottom.

SSCHLUNK!

Inside was his Utility Belt with all his crime-fighting gear and weapons. Now he had what he needed.

The prisoners of Squad A rushed in through the kitchen doors. Batman threw a Batarang and shielded his eyes.

BA-BANG!

The flash of light was blinding. "Argh!" cried the prisoners, covering their eyes.

Batman knew they'd regain their eyesight in a few seconds. That was all the time he needed.

The Dark Knight quickly took another Batarang out from his Utility Belt and threw it over the thugs.

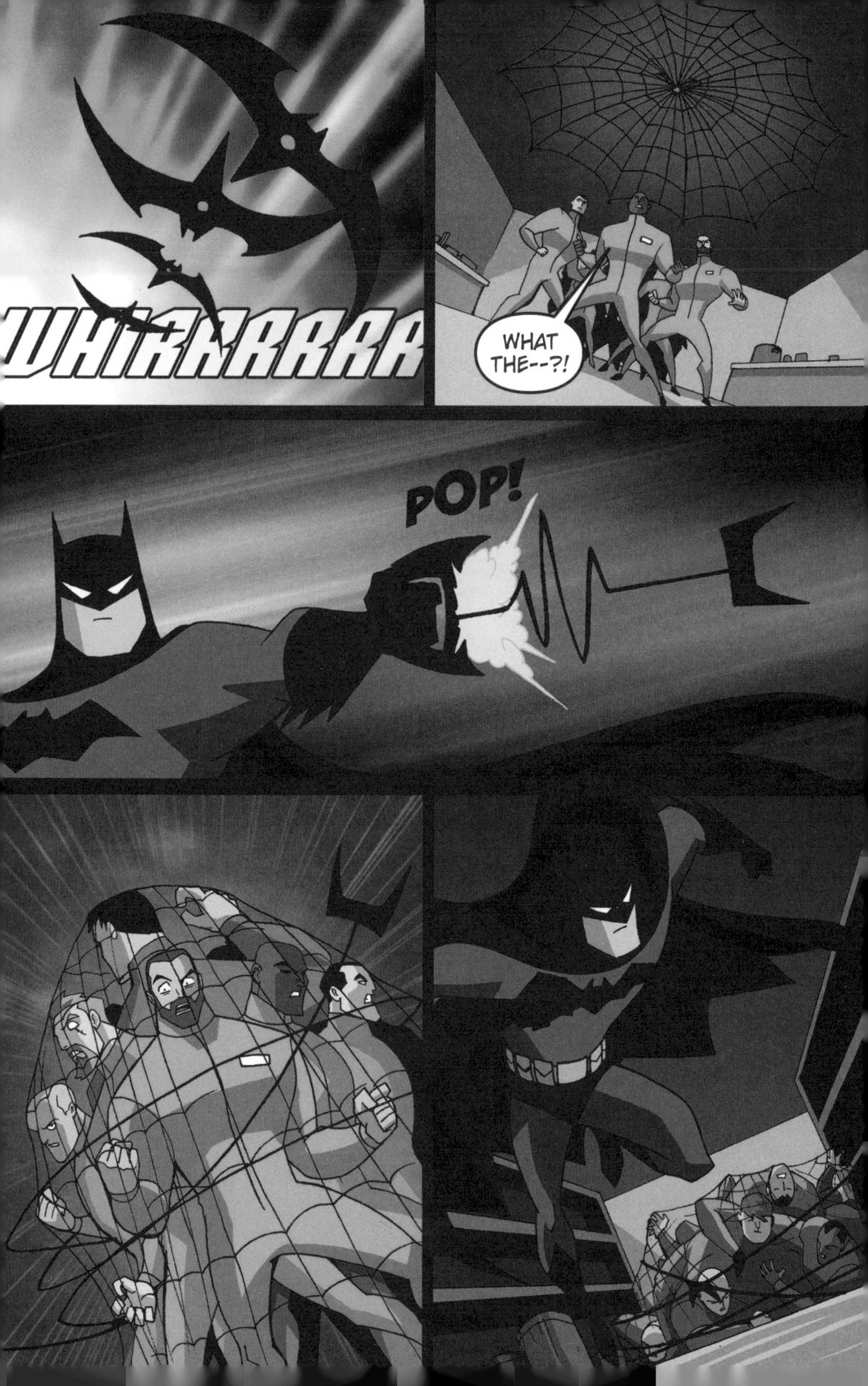
WHIRRRRRR
WHAT THE--?!
POP!

The Dark Knight raced past them and wrapped the cord around them once, then tied it to the door of the storeroom. Then he ran through the kitchen and into the giant hall that held all the cells.

There he found the Penguin and the Warden waiting for him. Behind them was the rest of the Penguin's criminal army of prisoners and guards!

"I don't know what you think you're doing here, Batman!" screeched the Penguin. Then he sniffed the air. "Or why you smell like refried beans! But neither matters! You think you're so clever, don't you? You smashed the gate controls with Batmobile!"

Batman nodded. "The police are on their way," he said. "And you aren't going anywhere."

"But when the police arrive," snarled the Penguin, "they'll find you destroyed! You don't stand a chance against an army! You're just one man."

"Not one man," growled the Dark Knight. "One Batman." Then he rushed at the Penguin's army!

"Attack!" the Penguin ordered his men.

The Penguin commanded the guards and prisoners like a general commanding an army. He ordered two squads to charge Batman from the left. Two more were told to attack from the right.

It appeared that Batman was going to be crushed . . . until he grabbed a Smoke Batarang from his Utility Belt and tossed it.

TSSSSSSS!

Smoke spat out of the Batarang as it flew over the Penguin's head.

WHISH-WHISH-WHISH!

The smoke set off the sprinklers, causing foamy water to rain down from the sprinklers in the ceiling. The water instantly made the floor a slippery mess.

SLUPP!
SLIP!
THUMP!

The inmates rushing at Batman slipped and fell on the slick floor. A few tried to get back up, only to tumble back to the ground.

While the prisoners' shoes were standard issue and thin soled, Batman's boots were thick soled and had deep grooves on the bottoms. They enabled him to run across the slimy surface without worrying about slipping.

All the smoke made it hard for the Penguin to see where Batman was, which made it impossible to direct his troops where to attack. Since the criminals had been trained to obey the Penguin's orders, they just waited for him to tell them what to do.

"Squad D," the Penguin began. Then he stopped. He asked the Warden, who was standing next to him. The Warden shrugged.

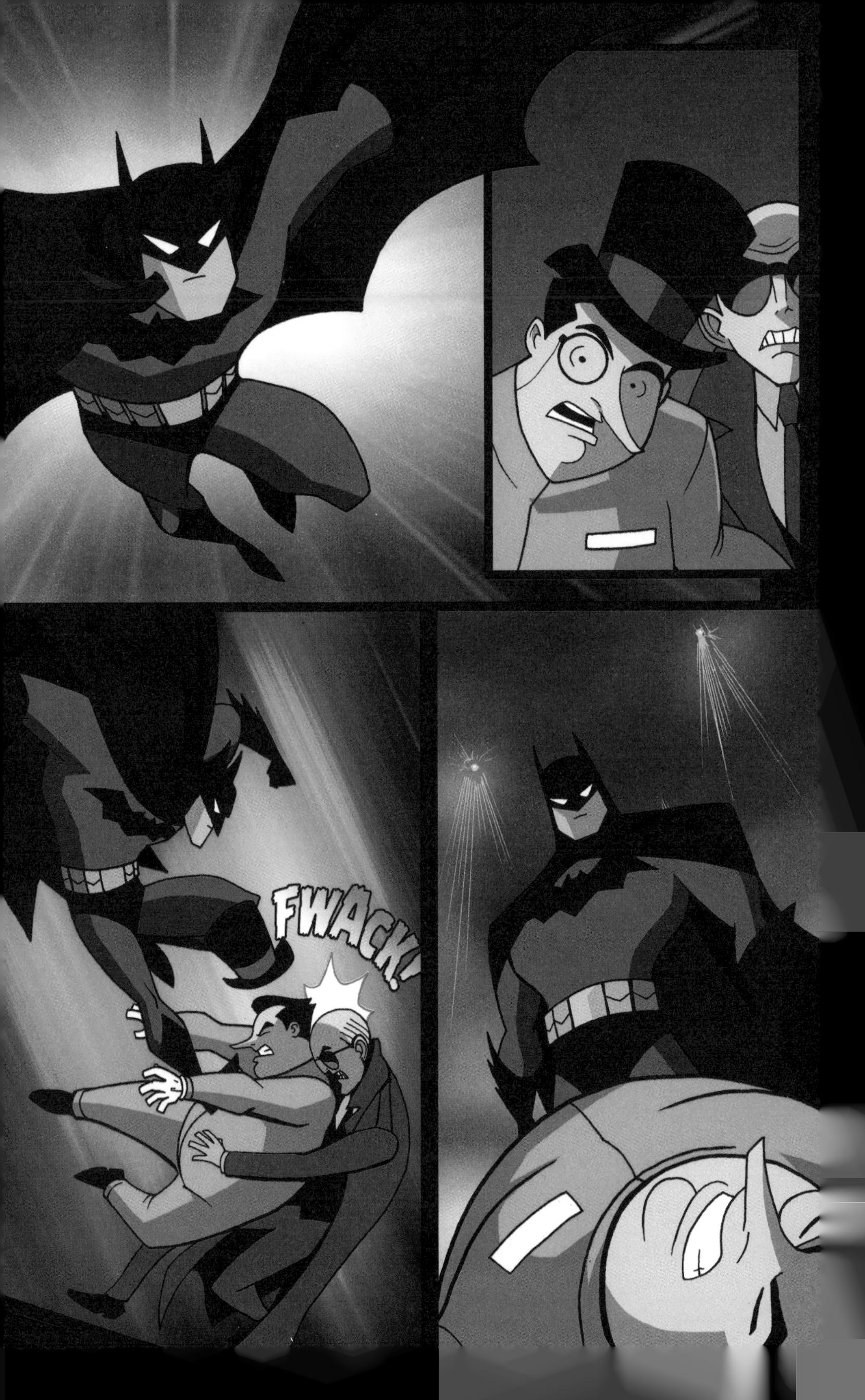
FWACK!

Without the Penguin to give them orders, the prisoners and guards looked confused.

"What do we do?!" one asked.

Batman used the moment of confusion to charge at the criminals. Two stood up to him, but Batman knocked them down with a kick.

OOOMPH!

The inmates fell backward, knocking several others against some nearby cell bars.

CLANG!

Batman already had an Electric Batarang in his hand. He threw it hard.

Z-Z-Z-Z-ZAP!

It hit the cell bars and released an electrical jolt that flowed through the metal and electrocuted the prisoners. They fell to the floor, unconscious. The rest of the prisoners and guards fled in a confused panic.

The battle was over.

* * *

A short time later, Commissioner Gordon and his police force arrived at the prison.

CRASH!

It took them a while, but eventually they broke through the thick front gate.

Once inside, they found Batman and the Batmobile gone. Everyone else was locked up in the cells, including the Penguin, the Warden, and all the guards.

As well as Bruce Wayne!

Just then, the Commissioner got a call on his cell phone.

"Hello?" the Commissioner answered.

"This is Batman!" growled the Dark Knight over the phone. Gordon didn't know, but Bruce had pre-recorded the call from the Batmobile after he had hidden it and his costume outside the prison.

"Bruce Wayne is innocent," the Commissioner heard Batman say. "He was working with me in secret. I needed someone inside the prison to find out the truth about what was going on."

Gordon frowned. "But why Bruce Wayne?" he asked.

"Mr. Wayne discovered that the Penguin owned this prison and was using it to train an army of criminals," Batman said. "He was in a unique position to be taken seriously if he were thrown in jail. He volunteered to get inside and stop the Penguin before his army could get out."

All of that was true. Bruce Wayne had done all those things. The only thing Batman left out was that he *was* Bruce Wayne.

"You trusted me before when I asked you to send Bruce Wayne to prison," said Batman over the phone. "I'm asking you to trust me again and let him go."

CLICK!

The call ended.

Commissioner Gordon pocketed his phone and looked through the cell bars at Bruce Wayne.

Gordon stood there, thinking for many moments. Then he made his decision.

* * *

An hour later, Bruce walked out of the prison a free man.

The Penguin, the Warden, the guards, and the inmates were all safely locked away inside.

Now that the Commissioner knew what had happened, he would make sure the prison was sold to a new company.

A company that wasn't owned by one of Gotham City's villains.

Because no matter what it took, Batman was
going to get all these prisoners transferred to
Arkham Asylum.

A *real* prison.

THE PENGUIN

REAL NAME:
Oswald Cobblepot

OCCUPATION:
Professional Criminal

BASE:
Iceberg Lounge, Gotham City

HEIGHT:
5 feet, 2 inches

WEIGHT:
175 pounds

EYES:
Blue

HAIR:
Black

Like the flightless fowl he resembles, Oswald Cobblepot has little skill in combat and doesn't seem very threatening. He is, however, a dangerous criminal mastermind constantly in search of easy money. Although he is one of the wealthiest men in Gotham City, few of the Penguin's proceeds have come from honest sources. Expect the Penguin to be protected at all times by a group of hired goons.

- Cobblepot's waddling walk and beakish nose earned him the unwanted nickname "the Penguin." His pursuit of wealth and success comes from the desire to rise above those who have teased him.

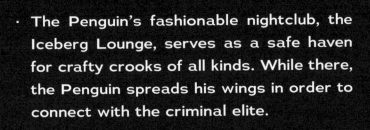

- The Penguin's fashionable nightclub, the Iceberg Lounge, serves as a safe haven for crafty crooks of all kinds. While there, the Penguin spreads his wings in order to connect with the criminal elite.

- The Penguin has a number of tricks up his sleeve. His special umbrellas can hide a variety of deadly tools. They can also double as a parachute or helicopter, allowing him to fly away from situations gone afoul.

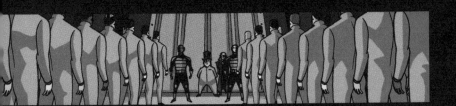

BIOGRAPHIES

SCOTT SONNEBORN has written more than twenty books, one circus (for Ringling Bros. Barnum & Bailey), and a bunch of TV shows. He's been nominated for one Emmy and spent three very cool years working at DC Comics. He lives in Los Angeles with his wife and their two sons.

LUCIANO VECCHIO was born in 1982 and currently lives in Buenos Aires, Argentina. With experience in illustration, animation, and comics, his works have been published in the US, Spain, the UK, France, and Argentina. His credits include Ben 10 (DC Comics), Cruel Thing (Norma), Unseen Tribe (Zuda Comics), and Sentinels (Drumfish Productions).

SKETCHES

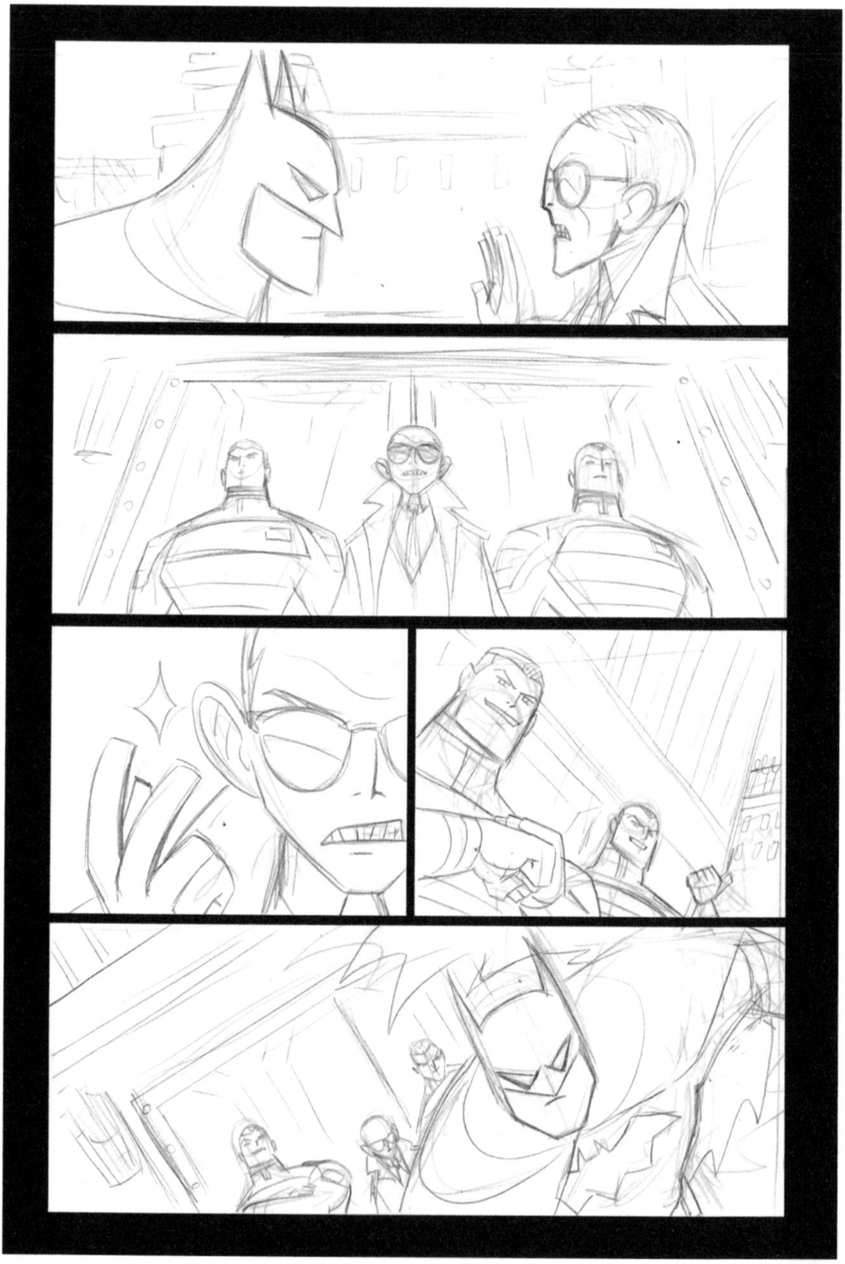

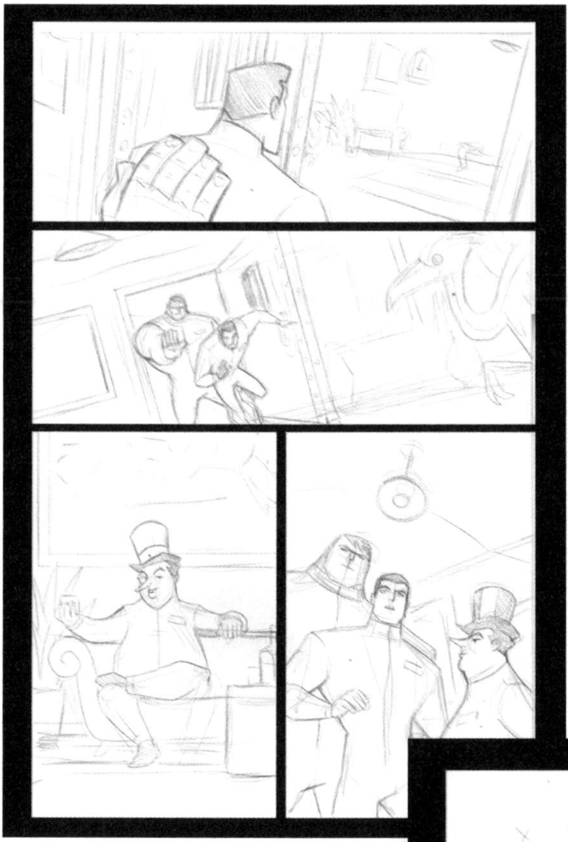
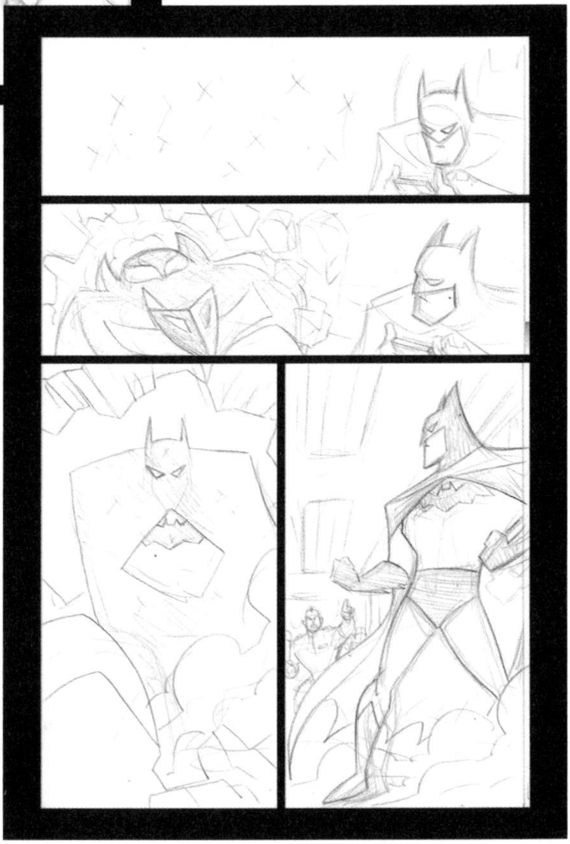

FINAL ART

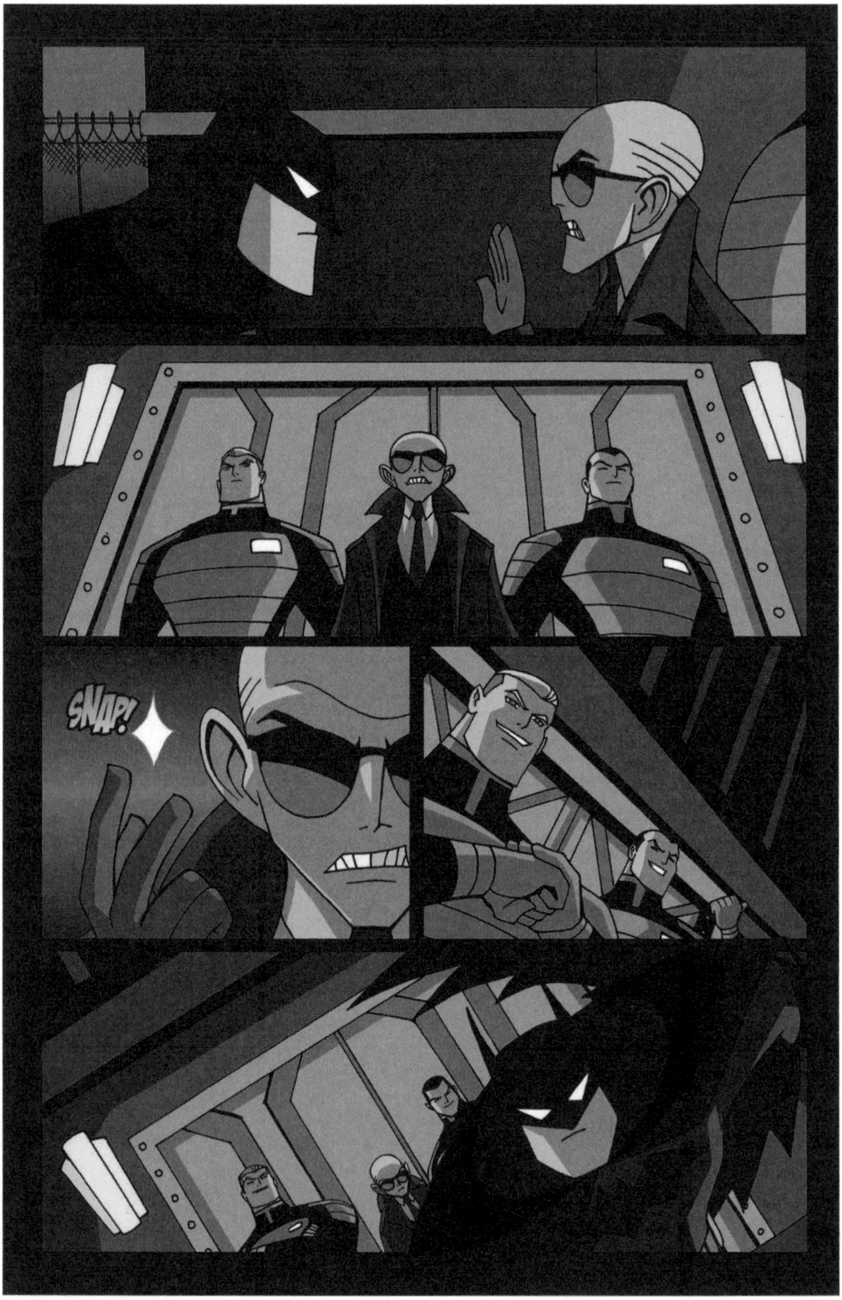
SNAP!

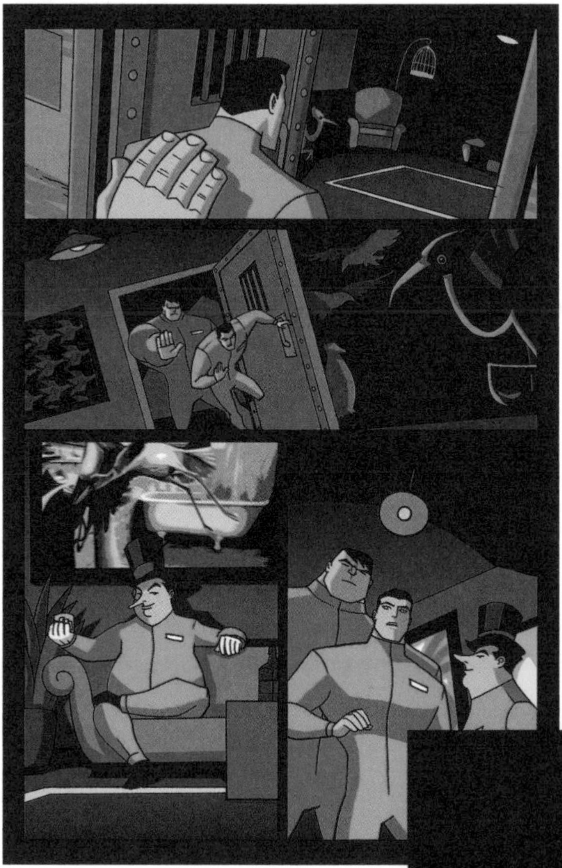

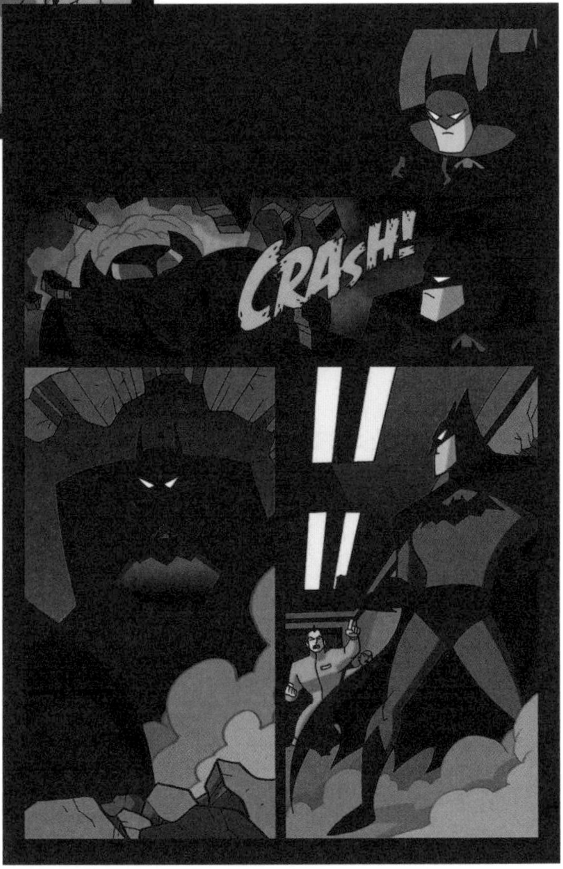
CRASH!

COMICS TERMS

caption (KAP-shuhn)—words that appear in a box. Captions are often used to set the scene.

gutter (GUHT-er)—the space between panels or pages

motion lines (MOH-shuhn LINES)—illustrator-created marks that help show motion in art

panel (PAN-uhl)—a single drawing that has borders around it. Each panel is a separate scene on a spread.

SFX (ESS-EFF-EKS)—short for sound effects. Sound effects are words used to show sounds that occur in the art of a comic.

splash (SPLASH)—a large illustration that often covers a full page (or more)

spread (SPRED)—two side-by-side pages in a comic book

word balloon (WURD BUH-loon)—a speech indicator that includes a character's dialogue or thoughts. A word balloon's tail leads to the speaking character's mouth.

GLOSSARY

asylum (uh-SIGH-lum)—a hospital where people who are mentally ill are cared for, typically over long periods of time

circumstance (SIR-kuhm-stanss)—a condition or fact that affects a situation

commissioner (kuh-MISH-uh-ner)—an official who is in charge of a government department, like the police

hulking (HULL-king)—very large or heavy

panic (PAN-ik)—a state or feeling of extreme fear that makes you unable to function normally

penitentiary (pen-uh-TEN-shur-ee)—a prison

retracted (ri-TRAK-tid)—to pull something back into something larger

riot (RYE-uht)—a large group of people behaving in an uncontrolled and violent manner

vulnerable (VUHL-ner-uh-buhl)—in a position where you can be easily hurt or harmed

VISUAL QUESTIONS

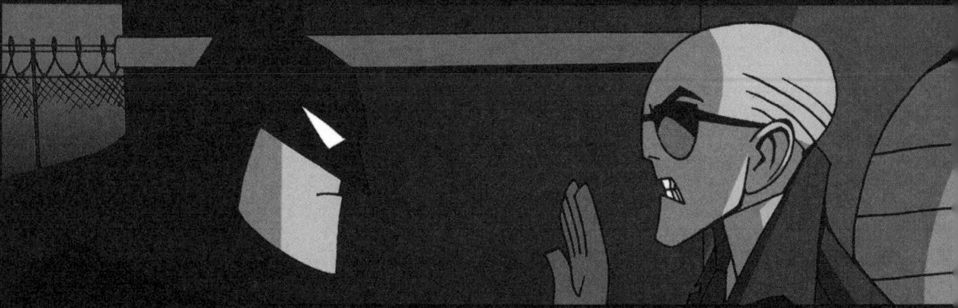

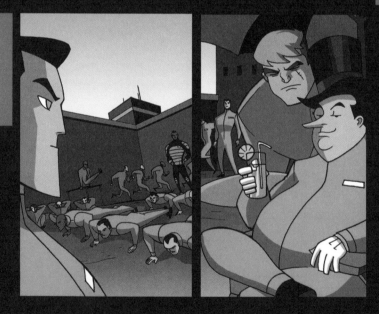

1. Why does the Warden stop Batman from entering his prison? What secrets does he have to hide? Go through the story and identify the crimes the Warden has committed.

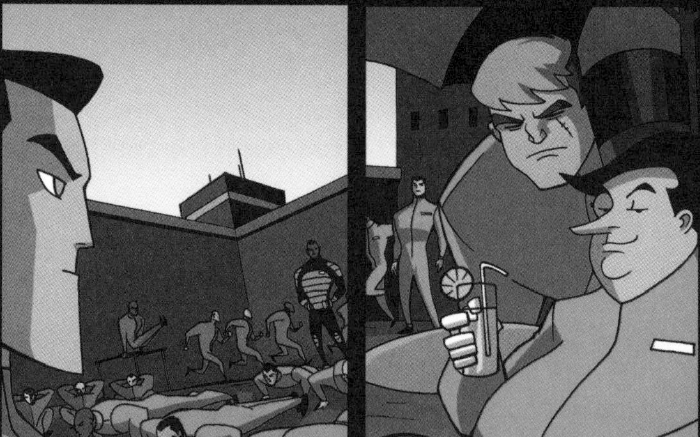

2. On the left, we see inmates doing calisthenics. On the right, we see the Penguin relaxing. Compare these two images. What do they tell you about the situation in the prison?

3. Batman emerges from his solitary cell by crashing the Batmobile through the wall. List the steps in order of occurrence that allowed Batman to make his escape, starting with getting his hands on the Batmobile's remote control.

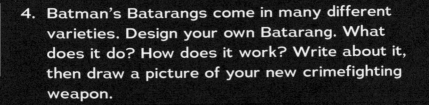

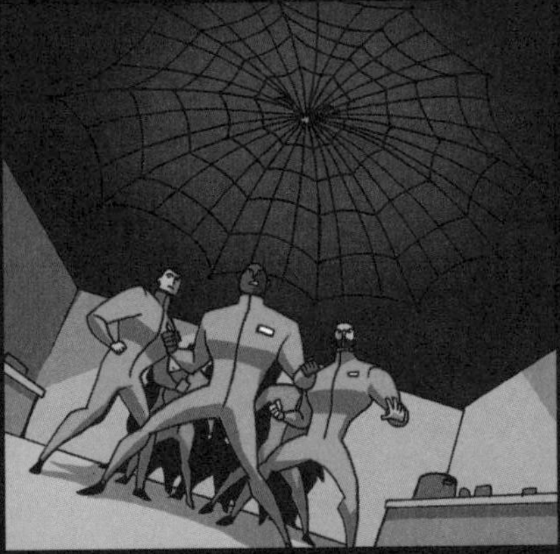

4. Batman's Batarangs come in many different varieties. Design your own Batarang. What does it do? How does it work? Write about it, then draw a picture of your new crimefighting weapon.